About the Author

Books have always had a special place in my life. I'm a classic bookworm. Swallowing an entire book overnight. Buying new books when the shelf is overflowing with books I haven't read yet. Reading the first part of a series and then waiting in withdrawal for the sequel. To dream that one of my favourite books will be filmed after all and then to say with a clever look: "It was better in the book!" It's all about me. It was after being inspired by all the books I'd read that I decided to try and create my own story.

My Violet Mate

Helen Polsi

My Violet Mate

Pegasus

PEGASUS PAPERBACK

© Copyright 2024
Helen Polsi

A CIP catalogue record for this title is
available from the British Library.

ISBN 978 1 80468 062 9

*Pegasus is an imprint of
Pegasus Elliot Mackenzie Publishers Ltd.*
www.pegasuspublishers.com

First Published in 2024

**Pegasus
Sheraton House Castle Park
Cambridge England**

Printed & Bound in Great Britain

Dedicated to all who love violets, werewolves, witches and parallels…

My Violet Mate saw the light of day thanks to the efforts of the super team at Pegasus Publishers, from editors to promoters. Thank you so much! Thank you to those who have always been there for me. Thank you for believing in me, sometimes even more than myself: my mom, Valentine, Asia, Alex, Lucy, Lacey, Anastasia, the Gantuch family, Aunt Lana and Bob… And, of course, my beloved Daddy (unfortunately, you are no longer with us, but I believe that you are always there and proud of your daughter successes). But definitely some of the most important words of thanks to my readers. None of this would be possible without you, my dear ones.

FOREWORD

The black wolf flashed his bright blue eyes, surveyed the street in every direction, and ducked across the street faster than a shadow, running around the corner of the pub. For a moment he looked up to the moon, which peered bashfully out from behind the grey clouds, shook himself off as if he had water on his fur...

A few minutes later, a young man came around the corner with a confident gait. A black T-shirt covered his broad shoulders, and an ornate tattoo on his right arm descended to the palm of his hand. His gait was smooth and confident, and he was united with the wolf who had recently run across the street by his tar-black hair and bright blue eyes. Or rather, it was he, Daniel Byne, who was the wolf. In the backyard of the pub he turned back into a man, to cross the threshold of the pub in human form...

CHAPTER 1

"How Werewolves Have Fun."

I looked around, making sure no one saw me. It wasn't that the residents of Blackbrow weren't seeing werewolves… The Defense Department didn't encourage such open appeals. They were the ones I worked for. At the department, in the special forces division. Blackbrow was a small military town south of Adamantha. Right on the coast of the Dark Sea. Virtually every family in Blackbrow had something to do with the Defense Department. In the sense that most of the town's residents, in one way or another, were connected to the military. Some continued to work to this day, some retired and went into simple 'mundane' business… But every one of them was connected to the ministry.

Adamantha was generally an interesting country, despite its small size. Surprisingly, in a small number of square meters, there were so many unusual things that an ordinary person would go insane if he knew what was really going on in Adamantha. Our country as a whole, and several cities in particular, have long been famous for increased secrecy.

And the reason for that was her location. Adamantha was a sort of border point between our world and the world of darkness. In three cities, Blackbrow, Swamphorse, and Understone, there were three portals that served as the gateway between the worlds. Between them, these cities formed the circuit of the Magical Triangle. It was this that provided protection against the opening of the portals. The circuit was fortified in every possible magical way. And in each of these three cities, there were guardians. They were responsible for maintaining the integrity of the circuit, which was the main prerequisite for keeping the portals closed.

In Understone, the 'guardian' was the huge Devil's Rock. Of course, it was conjured and enchanted. All the wizards of Adamantha united to make the stone impregnable, and placed it right where the portal was. In Swamphorse, hereditary witches watched over the integrity of the circuit. And in Blackbrow, werewolves from an ancient clan of empathics provided protection.

According to ancient beliefs, werewolves have long lived in Blackbrow. They were noted for their incredible strength and stamina. Every battle had been fought in which they were known to have only two choices: escape or die. Werewolf warriors took no prisoners, and all their enemies were slaughtered in the truest sense of the word. In addition to their superior physical prowess, these wolf warriors possessed the ability to sense and read their enemies on another, spiritual level. But it was their true nature that instilled the greatest fear. In fiercest battles, wolf warriors transformed into wolves. This made them practically invulnerable...

Over the centuries, everything mixed up, and people gradually penetrated into the life of Adamantha's supernatural beings. We could work in the same institutions and even build families... And some even managed to leave their especially magical cities and settle in the central parts of Adamantha, where, incidentally, ordinary people prevailed, and modern generations were increasingly inclined to the version that all supernatural Adamantha – no more than echoes of ancient legends...

I looked around once more, making sure my little trick had gone unnoticed. When I didn't see any unnecessary witnesses, I grinned to myself. Top-notch.

I entered the pub. There was the usual atmosphere. The hum of conversation, the clinking of glasses, the soft rock ballads from the jukebox in the background... For a werewolf with his keen hearing, it all sounded much louder. But I was used to it. Years of training had taught me not to focus on it. Otherwise you could just go crazy. Just as I'd trained myself to control when I turned and to confront the full moon.

I looked around the pub from my considerable height. I saw Greg at one of the far tables.

Greg stared thoughtfully at the half-empty whiskey glass in front of him. Cautiously avoiding people, I headed toward the guy.

"Do you think you've had enough, or are you contemplating doing it again?" I asked, walking over to the table.

Greg raised his head and nodded to me.

"Yeah," he replied, "something like that... what do you think about that?"

"Tough question," I smiled, sitting down across from him.

When I noticed the waitress hovering between the tables, I raised my hand, drawing attention to myself.

"You don't have a car today? Are you going out?" Greg looked at me questioningly.

"Yeah... Is it that noticeable?"

Greg just grinned.

"There's a little bit. The eyes..." He nodded at my face.

"Shit... Again..."

I took a deep breath and slowly lowered my eyelids. One of the downsides of conversions has always been glowing eyes. And right now, my eyes were glowing blue. They were, literally, glittering in the half-darkened room of the pub. Of course, that wasn't an uncontrollable trait of werewolves. Especially ones like me. But not now...

"Have you noticed that lately, it's happening more and more?" said Greg, taking a sip. "It's getting more and more difficult to control the consequences of conversions..."

I ran my hand through my hair. Of course I'd noticed that. What's more, all the special forces werewolves were starting to talk about it more and more.

You could say that the reason for it was known, too. But... It all sounded too catastrophic for anyone to want to believe and accept.

"Do you think what they were talking about at the briefing today?" I sighed. "The portal could really open?"

Just then a waitress approached our table. The lush-breasted blonde smiled broadly when she saw me.

"Dany," she chirped, "I thought you weren't coming in today."

The girl playfully shot me her brightly colored eyes.

"How could I, Angela?" I put one of my world-seducing smiles on my face.

From the outside, it might even have looked like Angela and I were flirting, and our sympathy was mutual. But we both knew exactly how it would end. Another night of noncommittal sex... I'd get my manly needs met, and she'd brag to her friends that she'd spent the night with Daniel Byne, one of the best special forces men in the world.

Angela continued to smile radiantly and put the glass in front of me, leaning too low, as if unintentionally.

"It's your usual, isn't it? Am I right?"

"You're awesome, Angela!" I kept cheering this game on.

"I finish tonight at midnight," Angela leaned even closer and whispered in my ear.

"See you afterwards," I replied with a smile.

The girl seemed satisfied with that answer. Shaking her hips, Angela walked away toward the bar.

"What are you doing with them?" grinned Greg, watching what was going on.

"Don't be jealous, bro." I took a sip of whiskey. "You've still got it."

A petite, brown-haired girl walked past us. When she saw me, she smiled playfully and waved. It was a similar story with her. Mary, I think that was her name… I nodded back at the girl and sent one of my trademark smiles. Yeah, I didn't take girls seriously. And I didn't want a relationship, either. At least not right now… In my defense, all those pretty girls knew what they were getting into. I honestly warned them about it.

"No way… Fucking anything that moves is not my thing." Greg continued to comment on what was going on.

"Okay. Let's talk about my exploits later. There are more important matters."

I sipped some more whiskey.

"There seems to be a big mess brewing."

"Yeah. You should know about that…"

And it was true. If we are to believe what was said at the briefing today, Blackbrow, and Adamantha in particular, and after it, the whole world, were in grave danger.

In addition to the world people were accustomed to, there was another dimension. The Dark World, the Dark Kingdom… Different sources called it different names…

A hundred years ago, the forces of darkness, led by their leader, broke into our world. They had one goal: to enslave everyone, wreak havoc and draw them to their dark side. The attempt to break through was successful, because no one thought of protecting the portals at the time. An agreement was made between the worlds.

Back then, everyone treated each other loyally. Sometimes even people from different worlds had feelings for each other. And no one was stopping them from doing so. To this day, you can still find witches, werewolves, and other supernatural beings in Blackbrow who have connected their lives with members of another world.

But this was not enough for the king of the Dark World, Greif Volturis. Taking advantage of the total lack of defense, he attacked our world. The forces of darkness broke through at all three points.

It was a fierce and protracted battle. It was then that the werewolves-empathics entered the arena. A lot of innocent blood was spilled, thousands of lives were taken... But the werewolves' warriors managed to triumph.

The Council of Elders decided to seal all three portals. Werewolves and witches united for this purpose. To save their world.

Between the three points of the portals there was a magical circuit, which strengthened the protection and gave time if the circuit on one of the points was suddenly destroyed. The portals were monitored around the clock. Any fluctuation was scrutinized.

Immediately after the defeat, activity on the other side of the portal decreased considerably, and then completely subsided. There was a faint hope that Greif Volturis had given up trying to break through. But it was the calm before the storm. In the last month, the portal's activity had increased dramatically. In some places, there were attempts to break through. But the demons, the henchmen of Greif, were promptly eliminated by the special forces.

I knew this from the source. My father was a gate guardian. He didn't say it outright, but I wasn't stupid enough to realize that the situation was serious, to say the least. The moments with the appeals, the controls, the ambiguous words of the ministry representatives... We were prepared for the worst developments. But the biggest difficulty was not to sow panic among the common people. This definitely could not be allowed.

"Father says it's much more serious than that. In fact, it's getting harder and harder to contain the gate..."

"Do you think he'd dare do that? Again?" Greg sighed.

Werewolves had a longer life span than humans. There were still witnesses to that very bloody battle in Blackbrow. Fearless, invincible, experienced warriors, they feared only one thing: that all that horror might happen again...

What is there to say. My grandfather witnessed those events. He died a year ago. But after that battle, he often woke up in the night with nightmares related to that very confrontation.

"Lately, the ministry has been increasingly recording a weakening of the circuit..."

"Why?"

"That's the most interesting thing… They can't figure it out themselves and what to do next. It takes time to understand the reason… But we don't seem to have a lot of time…"

"But we're ready to invade, aren't we?"

I only grinned. No one could be prepared for an attack by Greif Volturis. All we could do was put all special units on alert and wait…

CHAPTER 2

"Operation Portal."
D.

The alarm clock was ringing nonstop. Without opening my eyes, I fumbled for the phone on the nightstand and pressed the button. It didn't help. On the contrary, the siren began to howl even louder. The siren... Stop! I opened my eyes sharply. It took me a second to realize that the siren was not coming from the phone. The howl of desperation, announcing danger, was coming from the street, and the volume was amplified by the wide-open window. I threw my hand off Angela's peacefully sleeping arm and jumped out of bed quickly.

At that time, the sound of the siren cut through the whistling noise of the fighter jet. It didn't take long for the short beep to sound. Quickly finding my jeans, I pulled a second phone out of my pocket. The same one the Defense Department had provided for everyone. The same one all special forces soldiers carried. The same phone that had been silent for so long. Because any activity on it meant only one thing: the portal is open, the circuit is broken.

Simultaneously pulling on my jeans, I opened a message on my phone. 'Operation Portal. Danger level 6.'

"Fuck," I cursed, snapping on the belt of my jeans. I just had to find my T-shirt. Somehow, inexplicably, it was on the headboard. Just as I tried to reach for the shirt, Angela hissed and rolled over onto her back.

"Dany." The girl's voice was sleepy, but in a second it changed and became frightened and anxious. "Dan, what's going on?"

The girl turned her head toward the open window. The siren did not stop. The alarm was joined by anxious shouts from people. No one understood what was going on.

"Dan, can you hear me? What happened? Where are you going?"

I finally got fully dressed and turned to Angela.

"I have to go! And you, just in case, gather everything you need: money, documents, some clothes and food... To have everything at hand. Close all the windows and doors. Try not to leave the house. Turn on the news and watch the messages."

"But... Dan? What's going on? I don't... Shit! Dan! Your eyes!"

I could already feel it myself. My heart began to beat faster, and the blood pumped through my veins faster. The intermediate stage before the conversion.

It wasn't that Angela didn't know who I was... The people of Blackbow knew they were neighbors with werewolves, but no one talked about it openly. There was an unspoken rule: no talking about it in public.

I slowly closed my eyes, trying to calm my essence.

"Do what I said! That's it! I'm off!"

Without letting Angela answer, I ran out into the street. I didn't have any feelings for her... She was a good girl, even if she was a little silly. It would be a pity, humanly speaking, if something happened to her.

I didn't have much time to think about it. I had to get to headquarters as quickly as possible. I didn't think much about whether anyone would see me, so I turned. And a second later, already a wolf, I was racing down the road, outrunning cars.

I decided to take a shortcut. I turned off the road into the woods, behind which was the headquarters. As I ran along one of the local paths, I heard the crunch of branches behind me.

I stopped and looked around slowly. The cold wind stirred the fur on my scruff. I flashed my eyes deep into the forest. A shadow flashed ahead, then another, followed by another... Actually, they were Shadows. Greif's court warriors. They would be the beginning of this bloody battle. I roared, trying to drive the Shadows away. But they were determined, and they weren't going to back down.

The Shadows were a blob of darkness. Shadows, in the literal sense of the word. To humans, they were dangerous by their invulnerability. By engaging with the Shadow, one was doomed. The Shadow could not be destroyed physically, but it could strike a devastating blow, sucking the life out of a man.

But that applied to ordinary werewolves, too. No one could put up an equal fight against the Shadows. No one but werewolves-empathics. Only we could make the Shadows vulnerable. Our strike was fatal to them.

Of course, I knew that. I focused my gaze on one of the Shadows. I had no time to think about it. I jumped up to the Shadow in a flash, and slashed at it with my claws in flight.

With a terrifying screech, the Shadow was blown to dust. Without hesitation, I did the same to the other two. One by one they scattered, but the last of them caught my belt. I growled in pain and rage at the same time. The wounds the Shadow had inflicted took a little longer to heal and were more painful.

I ran out of the forest and stood in front of the headquarters gate. In a second, I was already in human form. I pushed the bell button on the gate, ignoring the glowing eyes.

The wound still hurt. I lifted my shirt. The Shadow went right into the waistband tattoo, damaging it a little.

It was the belt that made empathics so invulnerable. The tattoo was transformed into a golden belt when converted. That's what distinguished us from ordinary werewolves.

Unfortunately, the Shadows knew of this weakness, and the first thing they tried to do was hit the belt. To shatter it and make the empath an ordinary mortal werewolf.

Holding the wound, I waited for the heavy gate to pull aside and entered the headquarters area.

The headquarters was like a big anthill. Ignoring the groups of people running around, I crossed the plaza and made my way to the command center. It was silly to see if my father was there, but I wanted to make sure he was all right. After all, the first strike had been against the gate. And if the Shadows had already made their way to the forest, I could only imagine what was going on at the gate itself.

I flew into the room, almost opening the door with my foot.

"Mr. Byne." My arrival was noticed at once.

The man in the black suit was looking at me carefully, covering the surveillance monitors with his broad shoulders.

"I thought you'd be faster." The man's lips tightened into a slight chuckle.

Adam Von was the commander-in-chief of special forces in Blackbrow, a special agent for the Defense Department. My relations with him didn't work out right from the start.

Agent Von was not very friendly. He seemed unable to fully accept that humans were not the only race of sentient beings on Earth. And the fact that werewolves were so much stronger than ordinary soldiers, he considered his own personal defeat. Von had questioned the abilities of werewolves and strongly disagreed with my being made the best fighter. Even though I consistently demonstrated excellent command of my superpowers in all my training exercises. Agent Von was looking for any inaccuracy in my actions. And now he's found an opportunity to hurt me.

Von's attacks always pissed me off, and I've never been indebted. But that wasn't important to me right now. I needed to know if my father was all right.

"What's wrong with my father? Where is he?"

"What's with the hysteria, Mr. Byne?" Von's partner continued to test my patience. "Did one of the best special forces fighters ever act like a flighty girl?"

"Listen, you." I flew over to Adam and clenched my hands into fists. "I'm not going to have this argument with you right now. Do you have any idea what happened? Or do you think this is just another drill?"

I took a step back and turned around. General Michaelson entered the office. He was followed by several more soldiers. Among them I saw Greg. My friend looked alternately at me and at Agent Von with bewilderment. One could hardly find anyone who did not know about our mutual antipathy to each other.

"General!" exclaimed Von.

I only saluted the general irritably.

Michaelson looked us over and sat down at the head of the table, nodding to everyone else.

When everyone was seated, he turned to Von.

"Report! What do we know so far?"

"We know that there has been a weakening of the triangle circuit…"

"Reason?"

Adam hesitated. I just grinned. Von's snark wasn't so perfect any more. He didn't have all the answers.

"We'll figure it out," Adam pronounced. "At the moment, we know that the most critical situation is at the Blackbrow Gate. But everything is under control. There are no leaks—"

"Got it," I interrupted Von unabashedly.

Von glared at me with an annoyed look. Everyone looked at me in surprise.

"What do you mean?" asked General Michaelson.

"Shadows," I replied, "at least they managed to get through."

"Where did that information come from?"

"From your forest," I hummed, "there were three of them. Of course, these particular ones can't do anything any more, but... How many more managed to get through, I don't know."

The general slowly turned to Von.

"How did this happen? Why didn't anyone react? How did they get here from the gate?"

"Let's ask the responsible... ahem... people about it."

Von smirked and nodded toward the many screens.

I got the gist of what Von was saying. He jumped off the subject technically, shifting the responsibility to my father. He was the one who guarded the gate.

I squeezed the armrest of my chair tightly to keep myself from lashing out at Von. Greg, sitting next to me, patted my shoulder soothingly.

"Right now, we have an opportunity to discuss this situation with Mr. Byne."

On one of the screens, after a brief interruption, an image of my father appeared. I breathed a sigh of relief. At least he was alive and in one piece.

The situation was much worse. The portal is open, the circuit is broken. Grey Volturis is building up his troops to seize the moment and attack. It seems that his plan was to capture Blackbrow and take control of the local portal. And the Shadows I met were just the beginning...

When the video call ended, Von spoke again.

"We have decided to reinforce the defense of all three points of the triangle. Aerial control teams have already flown out to Swamphorse and Understone. This—"

"That's nonsense." I couldn't stand it. "Don't you see that this is about something else entirely! We don't need aviation and infantry here! Do you realize who you're dealing with? He doesn't care about your planes and tanks!"

"Mr. Byne, show some respect," Von tried to sass me, "change your tone in the presence of the general!"

"Oh, that's—"

"Stand down!"

Michaelson intervened in our quarrel. Everyone was abruptly silent. The general looked around with a stern look.

"Carry on, Byne." He nodded to me.

Von only pursed his lips in annoyance.

"We have to fight them with their methods," I went on to say, "we need to find out why the circuit weakened, repair the leak, and seal the portal. That's the only way we can prevent an attack. And weapons won't help here. This isn't a human war…"

"Your strategy?"

"As I said, we need to figure out why the circuit was broken…"

In the course of long discussions, it was decided to create two reconnaissance groups: to Swamphorse and to Understone. In order not to attract unnecessary attention, a group of three werewolves, led by Greg, was sent to Understone. As for Swamphorse… General Michaelson thought I could handle the mission alone. The rest of the special forces were immediately redeployed to the gate. After all, they were the only ones who could fight back adequately in the event of a full-scale attack.

Of course, I wanted to come to my father's aid and stand shoulder to shoulder with him in defense of Blackbrow. But… management orders were not a topic for discussion. I consoled myself with the hope that, despite his age, Mr. Byne Senior had not yet lost his werewolf-like powers, and would stand firm in defense of the gate…

CHAPTER 3

"Take Care of Her."
D.

The day passed in quiet tension. The Shadows no longer tried to break through. But the portal continued to be weak. The threat of a breach still remained. And that tense silence was even more frightening. No one could predict what Greif had in mind, or when the next attack would come.

I never got to see my father, but I did talk to him on the phone. Of course, I knew it was hardly all good. But his voice was pretty calm. Really... It would have been strange to hear him throwing tantrums and screaming, of the 'it's all gone' variety, but still...

I didn't know how long my trip to Swamphorse would take, but I decided to limit myself to a small bag of essentials. I could ignore everything and get there by turning. Werewolves have decent speed. But turning, and running like that, is not a bad thing. I didn't know what I'd be up against, so I thought I'd save my strength. Besides, Von admonished me not to draw too much attention to myself. The half-wit was right about one thing. A wolf running down the highway would create more excitement than a guy in a car.

It was about a four-hour drive to Swamphorse. But at four in the morning, I was all ready and on my way. Start early, finish early...

Though... I had to admit, when I left for Swamphorse, I had no idea when I would be back. Would I ever come back?

Shadows were flying over Blackbrow. Yes, they didn't come down on the ground, didn't attack people... They just circled over the city in a dark, scary mass... It was further proof that the circuit was weakened. At such moments, the sky above Adamantha became more transparent, something like that... and we could see all the evil things that were circling above us. When I said 'we', I meant a certain category of people. Werewolves, witches, elders... They were the only ones who could see the frightening picture that Greif Volturis was creating.

After two hours on the road, I stopped at a gas station for coffee and gas. As soon as I got out of the car, I had a lingering feeling that I was being watched. Focusing on my sensations, I slowly turned around. The gas station was empty. There was no one else here besides my car. Being careful, I walked slowly toward the supermarket.

The feeling of being followed continued until I got onto Highway 79, which led directly to Swamphorse.

Finally, the right signpost appeared on the road. I turned off the roundabout onto a city road. The ministry gave me the address. Though I already knew the information. That was our story. All of the werewolves knew that Blackbrow, Swamphorse Understone was a place of heightened magical activity.

Though all three portals were securely closed after the first great battle, a loophole was created for who knows what reason. If the two portals, Blackbrow and Swamphorse, were breached, the circuit's defenses would automatically collapse. And the third, largest portal would open. And then there will be no obstacles for the king of darkness. The forces will be unequal…

After checking the navigator, I turned off into one of the narrow streets of Swamphorse. I'd never been to this city before. It was hard to tell what kind of impression it made. But I didn't have time to think about the sights. I hadn't come here on a field trip at all.

I turned off the engine and got out of the car. There wasn't a soul around. It looked like Swamphorse didn't like to get up early. I walked to the gate and pulled the small metal knob. With a slight creak, the rusted gate gave way. Before I entered the yard, I looked around.

I turned the knob, opened the gate, and stepped into the courtyard. It was strange… The place didn't look lived in. The once well-kept lawn was overgrown with tall green grass, in which, in some places, wildflowers peeked through modestly. The stone-paved pathway had sprouted green growths, too.

I went up to the dilapidated porch and knocked on the door. Nothing. After waiting a few minutes, I knocked on the window and tried to look in through the small glass sash. But I saw nothing. The window was curtained on the inside with a thick dark curtain.

There was no hurry to open the door. I pulled the knob and found that it was locked.

At a loss, I walked down the porch. Just in case, I turned around again. But nothing had changed.

I stepped out onto the road and stared at the wooden fence. Of course, I knew it wouldn't be easy. But I certainly hadn't expected the hardship to start so quickly. Yes, the door was locked. I could assume that the owners had gone out, and all I had to do was wait, but... I had time to scan the house. There had been no life here for a long time. Much less magic. No, something was present, of course. But the energy was very faint. It wasn't coming from a living soul. Most likely, it was the things that kept the memories of their mistress.

So why did the ministry send me here? Don't they know that this place has been vacant for a long time? That's probably why the circuit was weakened. The guardian was simply not here. Consequently, there was no one to monitor the portal. But how could the ministry miss such important information? Or are they not as powerful as they claim to be? Where would I go now? Where do I find the guardian to bring him back here? To the place where he should be... I must call my father. He must know something about this dark story...

I reached into my jeans pocket for my phone. But I didn't have time to make the call.

"Are you looking for someone?" I heard behind me.

I turned around at the voice. There was an old woman standing in front of me. She was much shorter than I. She wore a long, colorful dress, the flaps of which fluttered in the wind. She was also wearing a wide hat, from under which the old woman was looking at me with interest through her faded gray eyes.

I was about to answer the woman, but suddenly it was as if a cold wind ran between us. I looked at this old lady. Of course, it had nothing to do with the weather conditions. There were only two instances in which a character felt this cold: if there was a supernatural being nearby. And if it was a mere mortal, such a chill meant that death was imminent.

I didn't notice any darkness or supernaturalness in the old woman who kept looking at me with interest... The conclusion was self-evident. I felt uncomfortable. After all these years, I couldn't get used to the feeling. I always felt uncomfortable when I realized that the person standing next to me didn't have much left.

A mysterious smile appeared on her face. It crept up on me again. It was as if she understood what I was thinking.

"So?" The old lady asked another question. "Is there anything I can help you with?"

I pushed the tangled thoughts aside. Maybe she could really help me figure it out. In small towns, neighbors always know everything about each other.

"Ahem... Yes... I'm... I'm looking for relatives. We haven't seen them for a long time, the connection has been cut off. And now… My father told me that it turns out we have relatives here. It's just the two of us. It would be great to find out about the relatives…"

"Relatives, you say?" She squinted.

Yeah… Of course, it's rude to lie, especially to older people. But I don't think the old lady would want to talk to me if I told her a story about a werewolf looking for a witch.

"Where are you from?" my companion suddenly asked.

"From Blackbrow." I was confused when I heard the question, so I answered the truth right away.

"Blackbrow," the old woman echoed after me. "I don't recall Stefania saying she had any relatives in this town…"

"Who?" I asked, and I immediately felt like tapping myself on the forehead. I think I'm about to blow my cover…

"Stefania." The woman spoke slowly. "Don't you even know your relative's name?"

The old lady was not a bad person. How cleverly she tried to trap me. Okay, Dany, come on, kid, figure it out.

"I… Oh, yeah… That's right! I remembered. My father told me she had an unusual name. How could I have forgotten? Stefania! Well, of course! So what about her? Do you know where she is?"

"She's dead." The old lady threw a glance in the direction of the lodge.

That's a hell of a turnaround I didn't see coming.

"What do you mean? How did she die?"

"How do people usually die?" She shrugged. "They live to a ripe old age, realize they've completed all their earthly affairs and that's it..."

Having said this, she raised her head and looked up at the cloudless sky.

"But..." I tried to latch on to anything. "After all, she didn't live alone. Didn't she have anyone left? Brothers, sisters, children..."

"Daughter," the woman said quietly, "she had a daughter." She exhaled noisily. "And a granddaughter..."

I got excited. That's something. One of them must have inherited this Stefania's gift.

"Where are they now? Do they live around here somewhere?"

"They left. A long time ago. Gone to Quetown. That town seemed too small for them."

Yeah... While I was figuring out what to do, the old lady suddenly took my hand and looked at my tattoo.

The ornate bracelet enclosed a wolf's head, the emblem of werewolves.

"Interesting pattern." She stretched out, looking at the drawing.

A chill ran down my arm.

"Take care of her." The old lady suddenly looked me straight in the eye and let go of my hand.

And before I could answer, my strange companion had disappeared. Gone. It was as if she had vanished into thin air. Stunned, I quickly looked around. There was no one. There was no one outside. Only the wind was stirring the leaves on the trees. And in that noise, I could clearly hear the old woman's last words: "Take care of her…"

CHAPTER 4

"Lunar Eclipse."
D.

When I realized there was nothing more for me to do in Swamphorse, I went to Quetown. I called my father beforehand to see how things were in Blackbrow. Fortunately, the situation was under control. By dawn, the Shadows had calmed down. Night and dusk were the time of their activity. But the threat still loomed over Blackbrow.

On the way out, I called Peter and gave him a brief summary. I had no doubt that Peter would do otherwise. He immediately got into the problem and promised to check with his channels before I got there.

Peter was human. Half human. His father was a werewolf, one of those who crossed over into our world when it was possible. He married an ordinary woman. Under mysterious circumstances, Peter did not inherit his father's gift; he was born an ordinary man. The true state of things in Adamantha was never concealed from him. Perhaps that's why Peter grew up very inquisitive about all things supernatural. In particular, he always wanted to understand why, in his case, human genes dominated.

Using his father's name, Peter easily joined the special forces. That's where he and I met.

We became friends and even took part in a few DD special operations, but then life separated us. Apparently, Peter had completely satisfied his curiosity. He retired from the military and moved to Quetown. But we kept in touch forever. And I knew that in a situation like this, I had come to the right address.

On the way, I booked my own apartment. Peter, of course, offered to stay with him, but I didn't want to embarrass his girlfriend.

In general, there was a mixed attitude toward people like us in Adamantha. People were divided into several camps. People like Peter, for example, knew we existed, believed us. But they were cool with us. There were others, fierce opponents, who believed that humans were the top of the evolutionary chain. No one was going to exterminate us en masse, the reinforced protection of the Defense Department contributed to this. But such people were not squeamish about petty nastiness and condescending glances in our direction.

But there were also those who believed that all this was nothing more than legends and myths of our country. For example, they saw the wolf on the special forces sign as an identification of strength and courage, not that it was a special kind of the very real werewolves.

We tried to live a normal human life, blending in with the people. Some even moved to Quetown, the capital of Adamantha, or to other large cities in the center of the country. It was easier to hide our true selves in the metropolis.

But both we and the Defense Department were well aware that if all three portals were opened, no one would have any doubts. And even the most inveterate skeptics would have to believe it. There was only one thing to consider: compared to the Shadows and the rest of Greif Volturis' ilk, we were saintly...

And all the way to Quetown, I couldn't forget the strange old woman I'd met at Swamphorse. Her demeanor, her energy... It was all strange... Her words echoed in my head, "Take care of her." Take care? Who? Or what was I supposed to take care of? My grandmother had seen me for the first time in her life... What could she know about me?

After standing in traffic on the streets of Quetown for a while, I finally made it to the apartment I had rented the day before.

After settling in, I called Peter again. We agreed to meet in the evening. The long, tense drive didn't tire me out much. But a little rest wouldn't hurt anyway. I couldn't let my guard down now. No one fully knew Greif's sick strategy, so an attack by his mad dogs could be expected anywhere and anyhow. After a quick shower, I lay down on the bed to rest. But unexpectedly, I fell asleep...

Darkness slowly descended on the city. Quetown began to turn on its evening lights in the form of chains of lights by the road and illuminations on the buildings.

I went outside and tried to concentrate. Nothing seemed to be happening. In the midst of all the sounds, I didn't sense anything dangerous. Well, that wasn't bad. If the supernaturals who lived in Quetown weren't sensing anything yet, then Blackbow was holding back the Shadows.

I got in the car and started the engine.

Peter worked as a manager at a nightclub. That's where he suggested I meet him. According to his story, it was a classic nightclub: with go-go, crowds of euphoric dancers, and a sea of booze on the bar. Peter was lucky to get a job at such a hot spot. But Peter wasn't just the manager of the club. Knowing the ins and outs of what was going on at Adamantha, he created something of a secret fund. Supernaturals who had a problem in their lives turned to him. Or they just wanted to 'humanize' their existence. Peter helped them with jobs, housing, and other everyday matters. At least a few of them, he managed to get a job at his club.

He must have been on good terms with the owner. That's why he was able to do all these things. The proprietor of the club seemed to be of the uninitiated, the kind of people who preferred to believe that everything supernatural was an echo of ancient legends.

I parked across the street from the clubhouse so I wouldn't have to search for a parking space.

I got out of the car, crossed the road, and stopped a few meters from the main entrance. There was already a crowd lined up here, eager to have a good time tonight.

I looked around the building. The big sign shimmered with neon colors. 'Lunar Eclipse.' I grinned when I saw the name of the club. How symbolic. Strange, though, considering that the owner of the club, according to Peter, had nothing to do with supernatural beings.

As I stood in the crowd, so much different energy came over me. I was surprised to note that along with the humans, the supernaturals had decided to party at the Lunar Eclipse tonight.

Finally, I managed to make my way to the entrance.

The huge two-meter tall bastard looked down at me. Something flashed in his eyes. I knew this was going to be fun. The bouncer was probably thinking of a reason not to let me in.

I took a step and climbed up the stairs. The bouncer blocked my way with his huge hand. I raised my head slowly.

"I'm going to Peter's." I felt myself getting angry, but I tried to speak calmly. I didn't want to draw too much attention to myself.

"You can't pass." The guy still had his hand in the air, not letting me pass.

Not that I was much of a fan of this kind of entertainment. Werewolves had keen ears, so all the noises were perceived in times greater intensity. It was a little annoying.

But I have been to nightclubs. I always wondered what criteria those big guys used to decide who was going to have fun tonight and who was going to be left with nothing.

Now I couldn't figure out why I didn't like the big guy, but I already knew what was going to happen. In less than five minutes, I would be inside.

No matter how hard my opponent tried to hide his true identity, he failed. I already felt his energy. Moreover, I even managed to determine exactly who this man (not really) was.

Omega is a lone werewolf. He had extraordinary abilities. Also, Omega has always been easy to subdue. All he had to do was show him his power. Omegas have never been known for their strength of spirit. They were always the wingman, not the leader.

Yes, maybe it was wrong. I shouldn't have taken advantage of my position. But this dude ruined my plans, and I never liked it when someone disrupted my business.

I took a deep breath and looked up at the guy. I knew now that my eyes were radiating a bright blue light.

But beyond the glow, it was a call to action, a display of power, a demonstration of self…

My trick was a success. The guard's eyes returned a yellow light, which only confirmed my hunch. There really was an Omega in front of me.

Yes, perhaps, here in Quetown, he hadn't seen anything like it. Because there weren't that many true werewolves. And most of them were concentrated in Blackbrow.

But he couldn't help but sense who was in front of him. Instincts – it was in the nature of every werewolf.

"I have to go to Peter," I said again, emphasizing each word.

Something resembling a low growl escaped the guard's chest. His eyes missed the yellow spark once more. He pulled a walkie-talkie from his breast pocket and said, "We have important guests. Show them in."

Finally, the guard stepped aside, letting me pass. I tried to hold back a satisfied grin. Yeah, right. I didn't need to go into arrogance mode.

Inside, I met another big man. There were no incidents this time. The second Omega silently led me inside the hall and nodded at one of the tables near the stage.

I sat down in the seat offered. The guard quickly disappeared into the crowd. Yes, they obviously have a problem with politeness...

It didn't take long for Peter to show up. I was just looking at the stage where the go-go dancers were getting ready to perform. A friend suddenly came out of the crowd of dancers and patted me on the shoulder. I turned around and saw Peter's smiling face in front of me.

"Finally!" said Peter loudly. The music wasn't playing at full volume, but you had to raise your voice a little to hear your friend, "The Blackbrow legend has finally made it to the capital! How long has it been since we've seen each other?"

"It's good to see you too!" I smiled.

We hugged and sat down at the table.

"How do you like it here?" asked Peter conspiratorially.

"I see you've done pretty well for yourself... You've done pretty well for others, too."

I had already managed to note that the bartender and a few of the snooping waitresses were supernatural.

Peter followed my gaze and smiled.

"Yeah... you know my attitude about it... I can't leave them on the street..."

"Aren't you going to get anything for this? As far as I understand, the owner of the club is far from that..."

"Yep... Exactly... I'm making an agreement with them back at the foundation level. They know that any mistake will get them out of here. That's Archer's job. He walked you to your table. Yeah, I know about your kryptonite myself... Now let's get down to business. How serious is it?"

I sighed.

"More than that... Blackbrow has serious problems with the portal. It is very weak. Ours is still holding the Shadows back. A few have managed to break through... Really... They won't hurt anyone else..."

"The work of the genius Daniel Byne? Am I right?" asked Peter, smiling.

"What about it. It worked perfectly."

"But what happened? What caused the breakthrough? Why did the circuit weaken?"

"The ministry wondered about it, too. They sent us on a point-by-point basis to Understone and to Swamphorse. Judging by the silence of the Understone boys, Swamphorse is the problem."

"Because the guardian left his place?", Peter inferred from the story I told him on the phone, "but then why did the attack start with Blackbrow?"

"They know the special forces are concentrated in Blackbrow. It's simple here. Most likely their strategy was to defeat us, then easily open the portals at Swamphorse and Understone. After all, only Blackbrow has active portal defenses."

"So you think this Stefania has a guardian?"

"It couldn't be otherwise. If the bloodline ended with Stefania, the magic of protection in Swamphorse would be completely destroyed. And we see only a loosening of the circuit. So their power is still alive. That old woman said they moved to Quetown..."

"Yeah... the challenge." Peter stretched out. "After your call, I put out a call... To both the supernatural and my detectives I know. They're looking... I think we'll have some information by tomorrow..."

"That would be nice. You know, we don't have much time. We need to find the guardian and bring him back to Swamphorse. And the sooner the better."

"Otherwise... The prophecy will come true?" Peter again flashed his knowledge of history.

And he was right. It was in our best interest now to hold back the attack and not let the circuit break. Because the prophecy was the most extreme and global way to stop the darkness. But no one really knew what consequences it would entail...

While we were talking, we didn't notice how the show program started. The go-go girls appeared on the stage. Peter poked me on the shoulder.

"I suggest a little distraction." My friend winked conspiratorially at me. "The girls dance like goddesses. You won't regret it." He nodded at the stage. "And they can do a private dance for a fee..."

I followed his example and stared at the stage. It wasn't more of a go-go, in its classic form, where girls sexually bent over the bollards to the music. It was more like a show routine. Each of them seemed to be telling a different story in the dance. But at the same time, they intersected and made contact with each other in the dance.

I didn't notice that I was staring. The girls really knew a lot about seductive dancing. But it was one of them that caught my attention the most. Throughout the entire dance, she kept her distance from the others. And her movements... her grace would have been the envy of any cat. The way she bent, moved her arms and hips in time with the music, played with the audience's eyes, and kept a mysterious smile on her face...

I leaned forward a little, trying to get a good look at the girl. Peter obviously knew something, because our table was right below the stage.

"Mmm... a private dance, you say," I said slowly, catching myself thinking that I wouldn't mind being alone with this stranger.

"First of all," Peter elbowed me lightly, "a private dance is just a dance and nothing more... So get your dirty thoughts out of your head and calm your eyes, pretty boy."

Peter continued to mock me. Even though he was human, I sometimes wondered if he could read minds. Because my ideas about what I might do to this pretty girl were definitely not innocent.

I sighed noisily and lowered my eyelids slowly, trying to calm my heartbeat. Another empathic of werewolves is heightened sensitivity. The dancer was undeniably arousing a storm of emotions in me, among which was excitement.

"And secondly," Peter went on to say when he saw that I had managed to calm down, "you can't afford her." He nodded at the stage. The girls were already finishing their performance, "Don't even think about it. Anybody else, but not her."

"Why is that?" It sounded like a challenge.

Peter was about to answer me, but at that moment the music stopped, and the crowd erupted in applause. The girls bowed and huddled together and came down from the stage. To the approving shouts of the guests, they came down from the stage, escorted by the guards.

And at that moment something happened. I felt it.

I was hit with a powerful wave of energy. But it was different from what often comes from supernatural beings.

It could only mean one thing. The guardian was here, at the Lunar Eclipse. It was most likely one of the girls who had just danced.

I rushed after them, but Peter stopped me.

"Hey, bro, take it easy... I mean, I know she's hot, but I warned you that... Damn it, Dan, what are you doing? Your eyes! Hey, come to your senses!"

Peter shook me by the shoulders. I shook my head, trying to normalize my condition.

"He's here." Instead of my normal voice, only a croak came out of my throat.

"Who?" Peter looked at me incomprehensively. But then, it was as if an epiphany came over him, "Fuck! Guardian! Here? Are you sure?"

"Yes!" I ruffled the hair on the back of my neck and looked backstage again. "There. And it's probably one of your dancers..."

CHAPTER 5

"The Guardian."
D.

Peter froze. He looked at the stage.

"One of them? Are you serious?"

"I'm telling you, yes! We need to find her right away. I need to take her to Swamphorse."

I tried to go backstage again. But Peter stopped me again.

"Hey, Dan, stop! We need to think!"

"What's there to think about, Pete? We don't have time for this! In order to prevent a breakthrough, I must return the guardian to Swamphorse."

"Wait! You can't just walk up to one of the girls and take her away. Understand, even if one of them really is a guardian, she probably doesn't know it herself. You know how it is…"

"Muffled power." Yes, I was aware of that. Peter's words sobered me a little. "But… what can I do? You know time isn't on our side right now…"

Peter was quiet for a minute.

"I think I know what we need to do."

I really hoped his idea was really worthwhile.

"Our girls can dance not only in the club. They can take their program to different locations."

"What a loyal attitude." I grinned.

"Yes," agreed Peter. "There is that. If there's an opportunity for extra income, why not?"

"Yes, but…"

"Only dancing, Dan," Peter exclaimed warningly, "the girls here only do dancing. Keep your alpha male attitude to yourself."

"Okay, okay, I'll shut up… I just don't see how that can help?"

"I'll talk to the chief. I'll tell him you want to have a party at your house, with dancing… I'll think of something so you can see them all again and… feel them. And then… Then it's up to you."

I wondered. Peter had a point. At the very least, I needed to know which girl was the guardian.

It was a busy evening, so Peter and I agreed to meet tomorrow when he talked to his boss.

Peter did not let me down. Already in the morning he called me and told me the good news. Our con had been cleared. Today I was invited to a rehearsal. It was there that I would be able to get a good look at everyone and get a feel for which dancer caused me those strange feelings.

Of course, I was ready to snap and go to the club right after the call. But Peter cooled my ardor again and urged me to cool my mind.

I had nothing to do until the evening. Of course, the first thing I did was call my father. What I heard surprised me. The Shadows were bursting into our world en masse, but they weren't doing anything. They were just circling above us, as if they were teasing. No one could figure out what it meant or what to prepare for. Greif had declared his intentions so loudly, and now... It was as if we were all frozen in anticipation, but... But no one knew what to expect... This anticipation was filled with suspense and uncertainty.

The only thing we were sure of was that we needed to return the Triangle's circuits to their original form as quickly as possible. In order to do that, we need to return the guardian to Swamphorse. I sincerely hoped that I would be able to solve this problem today. I decided not to spread myself too thin, making excuses for the guardian to come with me. I would tell her the truth at once. And then... I couldn't get her to run away, but I could get her to Swamphorse. Even if I have to use force...

I drove around Quetown aimlessly, passing the time until evening. There was another reason why this portal issue needed to be closed as soon as possible. It was all affecting us.

I felt it, and I knew others felt the same way. Especially those who live in and around Blackbrow. The desire to turn. It had been present almost all along, ever since we'd learned that the impure had weakened the portal. Fighting our own natures was getting harder and harder. We were all supernatural beings, and the portal.

The portal itself was something "non-human." Our energies overlapped… That's why we were very sensitive in such moments. Even seasoned werewolves talked about the difficulty of controlling conversions and behavior in wolf form. What to say about new recruits… In one of the conversions, their animal essence could simply take over, the control over the human side would be lost. And okay, if the biggest trouble was that the werewolf-empath wouldn't be able to take back his human face. In the end, it can be fixed by turning to the Council of Mages and to the wizards. It would be a little painful, but possible… Worse, the shapeshifter could attack innocents if it lost control. And that would violate the ancient code of Werewolves and humans. And confrontations within Adamantha would only benefit the Dark Forces…

In this regard, the Defense Department was concerned about the coming full moon. For all werewolves, it was a critical phase of the moon. But the full moon, combined with the energy of the portal, could do something terrible. So the Prophecy had said. It was imperative that these two moments not coincide…

I did not arrive at the club in a very good mood. The closer the X-hour came, the more I wondered how it would go and how easy it would be for me to accomplish this mission.

There was no crowd at the entrance today. The same Omega guard was bored at the door. I approached him and nodded in greeting.

"I'm going to Peter's."

Omega glanced at me and silently moved aside to let me pass. I stepped inside and grinned. Either Peter had given them an educational talk, or Omega was too proud to admit his mistake.

Peter was talking to the bartender about something. The club was empty. Apparently, the main fun was starting here a little later. I walked over to the bar. Peter looked away from his conversation with the bartender and turned to me.

"You're just in time. Let's go."

He led me somewhere inside through the corridors of the club, giving me a briefing on the way.

"So, here's the deal. You want to throw a big party to celebrate your move to Quetown. You're opening a business here and you're so determined to impress your future partners."

I couldn't help smiling. Peter looked at me.

"What? I had to come up with a 'human' reason. It's not like I couldn't say, a werewolf is coming to see us today, to find out which one of you is the guardian…"

I just shrugged my shoulders.

"But sooner or later, she's going to find out the truth…"

"Dan," Peter sighed, "you got me…"

"Okay. You can rest easy. The legend is more than human. In fact, I have you to thank for arranging all this."

"I haven't done anything yet. When it's over, then we'll talk about gratitude…"

We came to the black double-sided doors.

"This is the rehearsal room. First we'll see how they rehearse. Then we'll have to go over some formalities with the owner. And, Dan," Pete hesitated. "I know it's difficult, but try not to attract attention… Make that diagnostic of yours as inconspicuous as possible… I mean… No bright eyes or any other visible magic. You know, we don't want to scare them off."

"I get it. Pete, let's get this over with."

We entered a brightly lit room. There were mirrors on the walls, a small DJ desk in the corner, and rhythmic music coming from a speaker. The girls were busy rehearsing.

Pete and I sat down on one of the benches. I tried to concentrate on what I was feeling. I fished each girl out of the circle and scanned her energy. I did it over and over again, but… But nothing… I didn't feel anything like I had yesterday. Nothing even remotely similar. Either the guardian wasn't here, or…

"Dan," I heard Peter say. "Eyes…"

Shit. I quickly closed my eyes and took a deep breath.

"What is it? Is something wrong?" Peter looked at me worriedly. "Did you feel something?"

"That's the thing…"

There was a question in Pete's eyes.

"She's not here…"

Peter raised his eyebrows in surprise. He glanced at the girls, then turned back to me.

"But you said yesterday that you felt it: she's here… Maybe you misunderstood something?"

"No." I was sure of myself. "It was definitely her. I can't explain it to you. But I'm sure of it. And now I don't feel anything like that... Surely it was all the girls from yesterday?"

"Yes," said Peter, thoughtfully, "I had to get to their rehearsal on purpose... Dan, why don't you try again?"

I looked at the girls again. I was sure there was no guardian among them. I was about to tell Peter that, but at that moment a familiar feeling came over me. I woke up and stared at the girls again. What the hell was going on? How is this possible? Either she's playing with me, or...

"Sorry to keep you waiting..."

Pete and I turned around at the same time. I saw the dancer in front of me, the one who had so caught my eye yesterday. The one whose private dance was unavailable. According to Peter.

Even though she was wearing a plain white T-shirt and jeans rather than a shiny stage costume today, I had no trouble recognizing her.

But as soon as I looked into her eyes, I felt the same flow of power and energy that I had experienced yesterday. It could only mean one thing: there was a guardian in front of me.

The girl continued to stare at me, smiling affably. I could barely contain my emotions. There was an incredibly strong, wild energy emanating from her.

"Ahem... Dan," pronounced Pete, "meet Lacey, owner of the Lunar Eclipse. Dan?"

Pete looked at me, waiting for an answer. But it was only when he looked at my face that he seemed to realize something.

Though I knew my eyes weren't on fire right now, as hard as it was to control right now. I must have had it written all over my face. Because all Peter did was look at me in surprise. All he could do was say one phrase:

"Holy shit…"

CHAPTER 6

"Why Do You Dream of Wolves?"
L.

There was an impenetrable fog in the forest. The wet grass touched my bare feet. The trees seemed like strange, bizarre silhouettes in the dense milk of fog. I walked through the forest as if I were cutting through a thick blanket of mist. I couldn't see where I was going. I didn't know how long I'd been walking. But some inner sense kept telling me that I had to keep walking forward, without stopping.

Suddenly a branch crunched behind me. I shuddered and turned around sharply. A strange shadow flashed in the distance. Silence fell over the forest again. I took a few more uncertain steps forward, and then an inner voice whispered to me, *Run*. I ran, obeying my inner impulse. My feet slipped on the wet grass. The thorny bushes whipped at my hands and face, but I kept running. I knew I couldn't stop.

I heard the crunch of branches behind me again. I heard a wolf howl somewhere in the distance. I turned my head toward the sound. When I didn't see anything, I kept running forward again. But no sooner had I taken a few steps, a huge shadow flew right out at me. I heard the roar of a wild animal. A huge black wolf was flying at me. A huge black wolf with glowing eyes...

I squeezed my eyes shut, as if my closed eyes could save me from the beast. A scream erupted from my chest...

I woke up. I woke up screaming. I was having a nightmare. Again. I don't know where I'd gone so wrong, but for the second night in a row, I found myself in a horror movie when I closed my eyes. That strange misty forest, the rustles, the wild wolf flying at me...

Yesterday during the performance I was haunted by a strange sensation. As if someone was watching me. I even caught a glimpse of the hall as we danced. Of course, I didn't see anyone. And I chalked it all up to fatigue, thinking I needed to slow down on the dancing a bit...

I almost calmed down and forgot about everything as I returned home. But that strange and scary dream disturbed my consciousness again.

Maybe I need a vacation? Or a visit to a psychiatrist?

As I pondered what my tired mind needed, I got out of bed and got ready for work. Today I needed to do some paperwork. I was so immersed in dancing that I'd forgotten all about the club's paperwork.

Besides, some important client is supposed to come over tonight. Peter says it's some cool businessman who wants to throw a big party to celebrate his move to Quetown.

I chuckled at the thought of it. Nothing changes. Men continue to go crazy when they see beautiful, seductive dancers. Obviously, this businessman is no exception. He couldn't think of anything better to do than book go-go dancers. Well, after all, that's our job. And the girls don't mind making a little extra money. Not that I'm stingy with my paycheck. But to some extent, I gave my staff, freedom of choice. No one could force them to go to the location. But they were quite active in expressing a desire to participate in such events. And our and Peter's task was to provide them with maximum safety. So that the dancing only ended with the dancing. I didn't want my club to turn into a brothel. Yes, I was walking a fine line, I knew that. There were all kinds of rumors about Lunar Eclipse. But despite the rather explicit shows, all the club employees clearly knew one rule: girls in the club only dance! And nothing else...

By the time I got down to the underground parking lot, I'd almost forgotten about my nightmare. My head was filled with thoughts of work. As I walked to my car, I wondered what needed to be done at the club, if there was enough alcohol left, if the equipment was okay, and what else needed to be ordered.

I clicked the alarm fob. For some reason it sounded too loud. The parking lot was unfamiliarly empty. A cold breeze ran down my legs. I turned around. There was no one around. But suddenly the feeling of being followed came over me again. It was as if I could feel someone's presence. I looked around again. There was no one around.

With a shrug, I got into the car. I guess I should really think about going on vacation...

Just as I was about to drive up to the club, Henry called me and corrected my plans. The paperwork at the office was delayed.

Henry had his own sewing shop. All the costumes we danced in, the staff uniforms... Henry did all the fabric selection and design. He and I had been friends for very many years. The day before I told him I wanted to make a new program and consequently new costumes for the dancers. Henry promised me that as soon as he found the right fabrics, he would let me know right away.

So now he called me and excitedly told me that a shipment of gorgeous specimens had arrived. Of course, I had to drop everything and go to Henry's studio. Otherwise, he just wouldn't leave me alone.

Henry was a bit of an odd man, head over heels in love with what he was doing. But I took him at his word. Henry was hardly the only person who stayed by my side at all times. When the terrible accident that killed my parents all at once happened.

It was a day that didn't portend anything bad. I woke up in the morning as usual and got ready for college. It was an important day. In the evening there was going to be a concert that we had been preparing since the beginning of the year. We had come up with the best dance and we wanted to show it to the audience as soon as possible.

Mom and Dad were also supposed to come to the concert in the evening. But time passed, we had our last rehearsal and were already backstage. I called my parents several times, but even then none of them answered the phone. I was nervous, but I went on stage anyway. The performance was perfect. The audience erupted in applause. And then... After the show, the teacher came to me at and told me that my parents had been in a car accident. They had crashed. Both of them. No one had a chance. The world stopped existing then. It went dark and empty. And then the darkness consumed me. The teacher's words were the last thing I remembered.

Then everything happened as if it were not with me. The identification, the funeral, the cemetery... All of this is stored in my memory as separate frames. Frames of a scary movie.

I forgot about everything. I just stayed home all day. The first few days I cried and sobbed uncontrollably. Then the tears stopped. I just sat in the same position all day, staring thoughtlessly at one point.

I don't know how it might have ended if Henry hadn't come to my house one of these days. He roused me, forced me into the shower, made me eat. Then he lectured me for a long time that I was doing the wrong thing, that I needed to move on with my life because my parents wanted their only daughter to be happy.

It was Henry who suggested that I start the club when my parents' inheritance fell upon me, and I was at a loss, not knowing what to do with all that money. Lunar Eclipse was his idea. Henry, a lover of dark fantasy, vampires, werewolves, and other things, thought the place was destined for success with that name. He suggested I dance. I'd dropped out of college, but my body remembered the moves. And I must say, it became a distraction for me. All the negative energy went away in dancing.

Anyway, I guess I owe Henry my life. Who knows where I would have been if it wasn't for him. Henry was perfect. Attractive looks, great manners, interesting conversationalist... But... Somehow it seemed to me that girls weren't interested in him at all. At least, I never saw him with girls. And I always felt uncomfortable asking him about his sexuality. Henry had always avoided that kind of talk.

I finally made it to the workshop. Mentally, I set myself up for a storm of excitement, parked the car, and went outside. As I approached the door, it was as if I felt someone's cold touch on me. I jerked and turned around. There was no one behind me, only the occasional passerby walking down the street. But they didn't care about me.

Shaking my head, I grasped the door handle and pulled the heavy glass sash toward me. The doorbell rang, and I stepped into the half-darkened workshop room. Henry must have been in his office.

My hunch was right. That's where I found my friend. Henry was standing in the middle of the office, gazing excitedly at the piece of pearl-colored cloth spread out on the coffee table.

"Hi."

I made my presence known.

Henry slowly turned around.

"Hello, darling. Finally!"

He flew up to me and kissed me on the cheek. And, without waiting for a response, he pulled me toward the table.

"Would you look at that! I can already see your costumes! It's not color, it's just magic! 'Dark Moon'!"

"What?"

"The color," Henry nodded at the fabric, "is called Dark Moon.

I just rolled my eyes silently. Henry's obsession with the whole dark subject was sometimes amusing. Henry was insane on the subject. He read every book about werewolves, vampires, and other things. As soon as new such films and TV series were released, Henry immediately subscribed to Netflix. The boy firmly believed that it was all written or filmed on the basis of real events. And the odds of encountering a werewolf or witchdoctor walking the streets of Quetown were very high.

Of course, Adamantha was famous for its ancient and rich history. According to ancient legends, our inhabitants lived in the neighborhood of supernatural beings. Some, like Henry, believed this to be true. And some were categorical, holding the opinion that it was all fiction...

Personally, I was neutral about it. Somewhere in the back of my mind I was probably of the opinion that there was something strange and inexplicable in this world. We humans simply cannot exist alone in such a vast space. But anyway, so far I hadn't met any werewolves or vampires, so it was hard to judge how I would feel about them…

"Don't smirk," snorted Henry, seeing my reaction. "You don't understand anything… but just look at this fabric!" He ran his hand over the cut. "Isn't it magical? By the way, I've even already done a few sketches. Check it out!"

From underneath the fabric trim, Henry pulled out some sheets of paper. Well, for all his weirdness, Henry was really brilliant at what he did. I looked at the drawings and realized how lucky I was to have met a talented man in my life. We began to look at the drawings, discussing the details and coming up with a concept for the new show…

I had been right to go to Henry's house instead of the club, and I had cancelled everything. Our process took a long time. After making a more or less final decision, I gave Henry my blessing to sew the costumes and finally headed to the club. After all, that rich client was supposed to be here tonight. He and Peter were probably waiting for me.

The club was deserted and quiet. After checking with the bartender to see which room Peter and his friend had gone to, I went there, too. The guys were standing with their backs to the entrance, watching the girls rehearse and talking about something.

I walked over to them.

"Sorry to keep you waiting…"

Both slowly turned at the sound of my voice. Standing next to Peter was a tall, broad-shouldered guy dressed in a black T-shirt. His face was framed by black hair, and his eyes were some unusual shade of blue.

"Um…Dan," pronounced Pete. "Meet Lacey, owner of the Lunar Eclipse. Dan?"

Peter looked at his friend. It was as if he had run into an invisible wall. He stood still and stared at me with his peculiar eyes.

Peter looked at Dan expectantly. I didn't know what was going on, either. I looked around me in my head. I didn't seem to be wearing anything weird, and my hair was fine… What made this guy react to me like that? What was wrong with me?

I looked from one to the other, still in a state of incomprehension. Meanwhile, Peter looked at his friend again, whispered something with his lips, and touched Dan's hand.

"Uh… Dan?"

The guy perked up, shooing the manna away from him and looked at me again.

"Oh, excuse me. It's very nice to meet you. My name is Daniel Byne."

He held out his broad palm to me. I exhaled with relief, realizing that the situation was beginning to even out. I held out my hand to Daniel. As soon as our palms touched, a gust of warm, even hot wind blew between us. I looked up in surprise to make sure I wasn't the only one who'd noticed it. My eyes caught Daniel's. For a moment,

I thought they glowed. Shining with a soft violet light. And then... It was like something flashed through my head. The last thing my mind remembered was a black wolf rushing at me. A huge black wolf with blue eyes...

CHAPTER 7

"The True Mate."
D.

No! It can't be! That's all I needed! I was supposed to be sent to save the world, and then what happened?

Yes, I found the guardian. There she is, in front of me… But… Maybe I was wrong?

The girl held out her hand to greet me. As soon as our palms touched, a gust of hot wind blew between us. I knew that my eyes were glowing like the lights on a Christmas tree. But there was nothing I could do about it. When a werewolf finds his true mate, animal instincts override self-control. The heat continued to burn between us. I felt a little dizzy. How was that even possible? How could a werewolf's mate be the guardian of one of the portals? What was I supposed to do with all this? How do I get her back to Swamphorse? And more importantly, how do I leave her there?

The girl seemed to sense something, too. Her frail shoulders twitched, and she lifted her head sharply to look at me. Something resembling fear flashed in her brown eyes. Of course, I don't think she'd ever seen anything like that… But before I could say anything, Lacey gave a silent groan and started to fall. I reacted in time, and in a second the girl was in my arms.

I wanted to howl, literally. As soon as I felt her body in my hands, the blood in my veins began to boil. My heart was pounding out of my chest. I tried to calm my eyes, but I felt like I was on the verge of conversion now. All my senses sharpened. I could hear her scent, squeeze her frail shoulders, and realize, I really wasn't wrong! I would only leave here with her! Under unknown and mysterious circumstances, Lacey, the owner of the Lunar Eclipse, turned out to be the true mate for Daniel Byne, that is me…

"Holy shit, Dan, what's going on?"

Peter flew over to me and looked at Lacey, who I was already holding in my arms.

"Come on, this way."

Pete pointed to one of the couches in the hall. Struggling with my feelings, I carefully placed Lacey on the couch.

The girls around us started hustling and came running up to us, too. Someone called an ambulance, someone brought a bottle of water…

I felt like I was going to explode. I had to get out of here right away, or the entire Lunar Eclipse staff would be watching my transformation.

"Lacey." Peter patted the girl on the cheeks. "Hey, wake up, Lacey? Dan, what did you do to her! Dan?"

Peter turned to me, but I couldn't hear him. I was hurtling toward the exit of the club. I was struggling with a huge pull. My true self raged and screamed. The beast inside me insisted that I should be there now, in the club, with Lacey. But the empath cold reasoning appealed to reason.

Once outside, I ducked around the corner of the club, ignoring my car. Thank God there was a deserted backyard. Not holding myself back any longer, I turned. Already in wolf form, I raced toward the dense trees that were most likely in the suburbs of Quetown...

I don't know how much time I had to run. I thought I had run for twenty-four hours. Only at the very depths of the forest did I allow myself to stop and catch my breath. I filled my chest with air. A second later, a howl mixed with a growl escaped my throat. It helped a little. I shook it off as if it were water and looked around. There was no one around. Thanks for that. Though... I didn't care if anyone saw or heard me at the time. After all, werewolves were not unusual in Adamantha. So what if people were convinced that we really existed?

I was sitting on the edge here, away from the city center, but I knew clearly that a part of me, a part of my heart, was still there, in the Lunar Eclipse. And so it will always be now. When Lacey and I weren't around. I won't be able to control myself completely unless I'm near her. Or rather, until she's by my side... So that's how it all happens... I hadn't thought about all this before. I was fine with a one-night stand. I didn't even think that identifying a true mate would cause me to feel this way. What am I supposed to do with all this? On one side is Greif, who is about to attack Adamantha and unleash his dogs on us. And on the other, Lacey. I have to get her to the portal at Swamphorse. But I can't stay there. I belong in Blackbrow.

If before I'd only had to tell her the legend of the guardians and help her access her power, now... I had to tell her what we were to each other... And now, the first option seemed much more feasible to me. In the second case, I wasn't even sure where to begin... Yeah... I'd be very happy with Von right now... A confused werewolf in the middle of the forest... It was a sight to behold...

Of course, I could have made Lacey. In fact, that's how most true mate stories end, but... I didn't want to... When I looked at her, I felt something... human or something... I couldn't take this girl by force... Yes, she made me feel a storm of overwhelming emotions, but I didn't want to hurt her... Something was holding me back...

***

I don't know how much time I spent in the woods. As I approached the parking lot of the nightclub, dusk was already falling on the city. I stood beside my car and sniffed the air noisily. Lacey wasn't here. Well, I guess after what she'd been through today, she'd decided to take the night off... Suddenly, a thought occurred to me. What if? What if I tried to explain things to her like they were? You know, the part about the guardian. Let's wait with explanations about true mates for now... Who knows, maybe I can awaken her power that way...

I got in my car, drove a few blocks away from the club, and called Peter.

It was as if my friend was waiting for my call, because he picked up the phone right away.

"Dan! Finally! What happened?"

"I'm sorry... I lost my temper a little..."

"A little!" exclaimed Peter, "you should see yourself! And your eyes! What was that?"

"I'm telling you: a little nervous breakdown..."

"Yeah, right! That's how I believed you. A nervous breakdown in a werewolf... Indeed..."

"How's Lacey?"

"Confused... Gone home... Said she wouldn't be in today... She told me she's been haunted by strange dreams lately..."

I pricked up my ears.

"What?"

"Dreams... It's like she's walking through the woods... And then..."

"Then?" I echoed after Pete.

"A huge wolf rushes at her..."

I tensed up.

"Wolf?"

"Yeah...Lacey says wolf, but..."

"What?"

"I think it was a werewolf... I think Lacey feels all those portal fluctuations, too. She just can't understand it..."

That's great! Does she see a future? A future in which I attack her... Great start to a relationship, Dan...

"Only..."

Peter fell silent.

"What else?"

"Dan, at first I thought she was talking about you."

"Isn't that so?"

"She said the wolf that attacked her had glowing eyes..."

I grinned.

"As long as I fit that description..."

"Yeah... Except... that wolf's eyes were glowing violet light..."

Unlike Peter, I was not surprised. Obviously, my friend wasn't that knowledgeable about the true nature of werewolves. But I knew... I knew why, in her nightmare, Lacey had seen the wolf with the violet eyes...

"I need her address." If my hunch was right, I needed to get Lacey as soon as possible and get her out of here. I was the only one she could be safe with right now.

"Dan, but... She's been through so much today already... Maybe you can talk to her tomorrow?"

"I can't wait until tomorrow! We just might not have it," I shrieked. "If this is Grafe's shenanigans, we have to go to Swamphorse. And the sooner the better!"

"But..."

"Are you going to give me her address or not!"

Peter was silent. I interpreted his silence in my own way. Without giving my friend any more answers, I ended the conversation and got out of the car. Well, I'll use my methods then. I looked out at the evening city, which sparkled with a thousand lights, slowly closed my eyes, and took a deep breath. I concentrated on my sensations. A light gust of wind carried to me an unobtrusive floral scent. Violets. Only these flowers have such a modest, exquisite, fragrance. Exactly the same scent, I smelled when Lacey found herself in my arms. I knew where I had to go…

CHAPTER 8

"The Shadow."
L.

Something strange was happening to me. As I drove home, I got the occasional shiver. What was it? What was this strange reaction to this guy? I distinctly remember this feeling of a warm wind between us. And then... Only darkness and that huge black wolf with unusual violet eyes. And that was it.

I woke up on the couch of our dance hall. Concerned dancer girls flashed everywhere. Someone was holding out water for me. In the background, I could hear a conversation. Someone was calling for an ambulance... Peter was sitting beside me, watching frightenedly. Everyone was waiting for me to react. As soon as I opened my eyes, I just felt a mute question from everyone present about how I felt.

And I... It was weird. But I was only interested in one thing. As soon as I came to my senses, I immediately thought of Daniel. I began to look for him among the others present, obeying some inner impulse. I didn't see Daniel among them, and that seemed strange to me.

Despite the loss of consciousness, I felt fine. My thoughts and the strangeness of what had happened, rather than my physical well-being, kept me awake. So I quickly packed up and went home, despite Peter's pleas to stay and wait for the doctor.

I tried to clear my head. I tried to figure out what was going on. What was the connection between Daniel and my reaction to him? Also... Of course, I hadn't told anyone about this, but I could have sworn on anything: I'd seen Daniel's eyes glow a bright violet color. Just like the wolf in my dreams... Could it be that all the legends about our country are true? Was Daniel some kind of supernatural being?

It wasn't that I didn't believe it all. Rather, I never gave it much thought. It all seemed so unreal that it seemed almost impossible to meet a vampire or some kind of witch doctor anywhere near here... Besides, in all the sources, for all these creatures, there was an unspoken rule: they couldn't demonstrate their power in public. Or something like that... I didn't know the subtleties, and I drew a conclusion only from what I had read before, and also remembered the stories of my mother.

So now I was wondering whether Daniel's eyes were shining after all, or whether it was all a figment of my exuberant imagination and I just needed a vacation...

Throwing it all down to fatigue, I tried to forget about the incident. I needed something to occupy my mind, so I called Henry and asked him to meet me at my place. We used to do this kind of thing all the time. We stocked up on goodies, watched movies and talked about life until morning... But, unfortunately, Henry was busy with something and offered to meet tomorrow. A little sad, I decided to have a similar therapy session alone.

I drove to the supermarket and began to throw into the basket everything that was always an essential attribute of our get-togethers with Henry. I filled the basket with ice cream, snacks, candy bars, and Coke, paid for my purchases, and loaded them into the car and headed home.

My spirits lifted a little. What had happened at the club was almost forgotten. I called Peter, warning him that I wouldn't be in today. After all, as the owner of the club, I could afford an extra day off.

I pulled into the underground parking lot near my house. As I pulled the heavy bags out of the trunk, I felt like I was being watched again. A chill ran down my legs. I set the bags on the ground and turned around abruptly. There was no one there. Somewhere inside, there was a subtle feeling of fear. Suddenly I thought I saw something flicker in the distance behind the pillar. Staring into the void, I took a few steps toward the column. Feeling like the heroine of a horror movie, I kept walking forward, realizing the stupidity of what I was doing. In those movies, moments like that didn't end well. But my curiosity was greater than my instinct for self-preservation. Actually, in my case, it didn't end badly. I saw no one behind the column. To be sure, I walked around it and decided to go back to the car. And there was a surprise waiting for me.

"Do you live alone?"

Standing beside my car was Daniel. The guy was looking with interest at the two huge bags I had managed to get out of the car. It was as if I had run into an invisible wall when I saw my sudden visitor.

Meanwhile, Daniel raised his head and stared at me with interest. There wasn't enough light in the parking lot, so I couldn't make out the color of his eyes. That was the first thing I thought of when I saw him.

"What are you doing here?"

Instead of answering his question, I asked mine.

"I think you got sick at the club... Came to see how you were feeling..."

I raised my eyebrows in surprise.

"Fine. Why do you care?"

Daniel shrugged.

"It's just humanity. It all happened out of the blue. Besides, I never had time to discuss my question..."

"How did you know where I live? Although... Peter said you were friends... Okay... I'll talk to him tomorrow. I don't think it's okay for him to scatter my information like that, I..."

"Stop." Daniel smiled. "You don't need to talk to anyone. I found your address myself."

"What do you mean?"

"Never mind. I have my secrets. So Pete had nothing to do with it. He even refused to tell me that..."

"But then how..."

"I told you, it doesn't matter. It doesn't matter now..."

"Now?"

"Yeah... I'll tell you about it some other time. In fact, I need to talk to you..."

I was even more surprised. About what? What did he want to talk to me about? I'd only known him for a couple of hours. And most of that time, I was unconscious. In general, I had mixed feelings about Daniel. As soon as I saw him, the feeling of incipient fear suddenly intensified. But at the same time, I didn't want to drop everything and run scared. It was fear. But I wasn't afraid of Daniel himself. I was afraid of what he wanted to tell me. So I decided to be careful.

I took a deep breath.

"Well... Then speak... I'm listening to you..."

"Here?" Daniel looked around.

I wonder... Did he really think I was just going to invite him home like that?

"Yeah. What difference does it make where to talk?"

Daniel grinned.

"Okay. Can we at least get out of the parking lot? I can help you carry it all." He nodded at my bags.

Without waiting for my answer, he grabbed my purchases and headed for the parking lot exit. I was a little perturbed by his hostile behavior, but I didn't say anything, just followed him silently.

"Well?" I exclaimed impatiently as we exited the parking lot. This guy certainly knew how to intrigue.

Daniel smiled, was quiet for a second, and then said, "This isn't a very common topic... I suppose you might be surprised... Very surprised... But... just hear me out. Okay?"

"What am I supposed to do with you? From the looks of things, you're not going to get away that easily..."

"You're very perceptive."

"Yeah... It happens sometimes... Well, tell me, what could you possibly want from me?"

"I could start from afar. Make a nice preface... It might be easier for you to take it then, but... It would take a lot of time, and there's..." Saying that, Daniel looked up at the sky. "We don't have much..."

"You're starting to scare me," I lied, because, really, I was rather curious. But I didn't want to show it so obviously.

"When I tell you everything, you'll know it's not me you have to be afraid of," sniffled Daniel. "Anyway, I wouldn't tell you a big secret if I told you that Adamantha isn't the only place where people live. I suppose you know that... There's a real threat hanging over us right now. Dark Forces have opened a hunt for our world. Greif Volturis has broken through one of the portals and made his way into our world. Now he has his henchmen scurrying around Blackbrow. Their main goal now is to open all three portals, to finally break the Magical Triangle circuit. Then we'll be completely defenseless. Adamantha will not be able to withstand the Dark Forces. And, accordingly, the entire world would be in danger of destruction..."

I listened to Daniel with my eyes wide open. I imagined what we looked like from the outside. To ordinary passersby, we might have looked like just a couple going home after a hard day's work and discussing how their day was going. But it wasn't that simple. Daniel was telling Adamantha's story like, it was just a normal conversation. About the weather, for example. From what he was saying, it appeared that all of Adamantha's mystical legacy was true, and not just echoes of ancient myths and legends. I involuntarily shuddered... Was it really true? I looked at Daniel. He didn't look drunk or crazy... His voice was quiet and confident. He knew what he was talking about. I also surprised myself. Or rather, my reaction. As soon as I heard what he was talking about, I didn't want to run away, to laugh, to say that it wasn't true... For some reason I wanted to listen to the rest of it. At least it would be an interesting story.

"I'm a little confused," I uttered when Daniel paused in his story. "I really thought it was all made up..."

"If only." Daniel smiled sadly. "Maybe it would have been easier to live then. But, unfortunately, it's true..."

"Okay, let's suppose... But... I still, I don't understand why you came? Yes, what you've told is scary... And if there really is a threat to the world, then there's a reasonable question of what to do to save yourself... But... Why are you telling me all this exactly?"

Daniel looked at me.

"You really don't seem to know anything... How is that possible?" he muttered.

"Don't know what?"

We had already approached my house. But I still hadn't heard the main thing. Daniel put the bags on the porch and turned to me.

"Every portal has a guardian. In Blackbrow, it's the werewolves, in Understone, it's a huge stone, and in Swamphorse…"

Daniel was interrupted. He didn't have time to tell me exactly who the guardian was at Swamphorse. Because it was at that moment that the wind suddenly snapped. It got darker outside. A shadow flashed near us. I didn't have time to react in any way when that blob of shadow was right beside me in a second. I felt terribly cold. And then… All I could do was scream…

CHAPTER 9

"The Scary Truth."
L.

My scream would have been the envy of any siren. But I couldn't help myself. As soon as the scary dark thing flew at me, I started screaming. The scream of fear overtook my thoughts. I couldn't quite figure out what it was. But somehow I was sure that the dark blob wasn't here to deliver good news.

But Daniel hadn't lost his mind. At lightning speed, he stepped between me and this strange shadow. But in spite of his speed, I could still see the way his eyes glowed. The same violet light. Daniel stepped in front of me, covering me with his broad back. The Shadow stopped, seeing that Daniel was standing in my defense. And then he roared. The guy who had been talking calmly to me a few minutes ago was now making the sounds of a terrifying beast. I put my hands over my mouth and stood there without moving.

I don't know what made the difference. His growl, his eyes, or his determination... But the shadow froze for a moment, and then vanished. It just vanished into thin air.

Silence descended on the street again. Daniel turned slowly toward me. His eyes were no longer glowing, but he still looked menacing.

"W-what… what was that?" I stuttered.

"How are you?"

I giggled nervously. Interesting question. I don't even know what to say to that.

"Who are you? Who… What was that? What was that dark something?"

Daniel grinned.

"I guess if you're capable of asking all those questions, then it's not all bad…"

"Are you kidding me?" I exploded. "Not only did I almost die at the club tonight. And now you're doing it! You showed up at my door, started telling me some supernatural heresy, then that creepy shadow… And your eyes… You… you… Did you growl at her?"

"Hey, hush… After all, nothing terrible happened… I think we should still talk… What if I told you that you caused this failed attack, in some way?"

"What?"

"Can we continue our conversation outside here?" Daniel nodded at the entryway door.

I don't know why, but I went for it. I guess my curiosity won out again. Or unwillingness to be alone after what had happened… Though… Being alone with a man (though I doubted it now) whom I'd only known for a few hours wasn't exactly a smart decision, either.

I sighed.

"Let's go."

Daniel nodded and followed me, remembering to grab the bags I'd forgotten all about. We walked up the elevator in silence. The whole time, Daniel's eyes roamed over my face. All I could think about was: what had I gotten myself into? Was I making a fatal mistake, inviting this strange guy into my house?

But the choice had already been made, and in a couple of minutes, I was already opening the door of my apartment, inviting Daniel in.

"Leave it here." I nodded at the bags that Daniel was holding in his hands. It looked like the therapy session was going to have to be delayed.

I stepped in, letting him into the living room. Perhaps I should have been a little clearer about the situation.

"I don't know who you are or why you came to see me… But… Let's make a deal… You tell me everything quickly now, specifically who you are and what was just in the yard. And then, you leave… And we never see each other again…"

Daniel smiled.

"It's not that simple. The situation is much more complicated than it seems. I can't just walk away like that…"

I had already opened my mouth to be indignant, but Daniel held up his hand, urging me to be quiet.

"I'll explain everything. And you'll see for yourself that it's impossible…"

"I'm listening." Okay, I'm not going to argue with him. Let him tell me first, and then I'll decide if it's possible or not.

"So, I started to talk about the guardians of portals, but we got interrupted…"

I grinned crookedly.

"Yeah."

I shuddered involuntarily, remembering the eerie fear that enveloped me when the shadow approached me.

"Adamantha is threatened, our world is losing its resilience against the Dark Forces. And all because the portal at Swamphorse has been left without a guardian."

"What does this have to do with me?" I was beginning to tire of everything.

"You are the guardian." Daniel didn't hesitate to answer.

"What?" I certainly wasn't expecting that. Well, let's get this over with. This is definitely delusional. Okay, I can deal with the fact that there might be creatures other than humans living in Adamantha, but I'm a guardian? Seriously? No way…

"It's true… I don't know whether it's unfortunate for you or fortunate, but it is. And now you have to go back to Swamphorse. If you wish, the world's salvation depends on your return…"

Yeah, well… It all sounds beautiful… But it's too much like a fairy tale… I can't be this guardian. And what do you mean, I have to go back to Swamphorse? Go back where, if I've never been there…

"Look, Daniel... Let's be honest. Just tell me that you wanted to hit on me and came up with this elaborate way... But let's end this game... You could have just asked me out for coffee..."

My words made him smile again.

"Sounds tempting... Was it that easy? Would you go if I called?"

Daniel took a couple of steps in my direction.

For some reason I felt uncomfortable. But I'd already told him. I had to get out of it...

"Yeah... I mean, no, I don't know... Why the questions?"

"Because I wouldn't mind... If anything... But after... We don't have time for that now..."

Daniel flashed his purple eyes at me. I felt myself blushing. He embarrassed me a little.

Satisfied with my reaction, Daniel continued talking.

"So... In the near future, you have to be there, or else..."

"Otherwise what?"

"I already said, the consequences could be dire. Besides, it's also a question of your safety..."

I looked at him with incomprehension.

"That Shadow we met downstairs... She didn't show up here for nothing... They managed to get to Quetown, which means that Greif most likely knows who you are..."

"Who is this Greif, anyway?"

"In our fairy tale, he's the main villain who wants to take over the world and plunge it into darkness..."

"Wow, a fairy tale." I stretched out. "Why would he want me?"

"That's just it. He doesn't need you... Alive."

Daniel fell silent. I didn't know what to say either. It was the perfect end to the day. Finding out you're being hunted by some crazy, evil jerk, and the only place you can hide from him is in some godforsaken town...

I wonder if all this is really happening. Or maybe I'm dreaming? Maybe it's all an illusion? Before I could think about it, I walked over to Daniel and touched his chest. As soon as I did, the familiar sensation of a warm breeze passed between us. I looked up. Daniel's eyes were glowing with violet lights.

"What the..."

I jerked my hand away and took a step back.

I didn't think this was all a dream. But... Suddenly, a terrible fatigue came over me. I didn't want this... Why did I have to take it at all? I was being chased by some weird guy claiming to be a werewolf. Then he started telling me all this crap about saving the world... No. I don't want to hear it any more. I want to go back to my normal life...

"Look, Daniel... This all sounds really interesting... But... I don't think I can help you... You're probably wrong..."

"I thought you almost agreed."

"You imagined it... Now I think you should leave..."

"You may not believe me, but you didn't even believe what you saw with your own eyes?" Daniel was in no hurry to leave.

"I don't know... It seemed... The wind... Something else... Go away, please..."

"But..."

"Go away! Please!" The hysteria began to come to me. "You come and start telling me some nonsense... And you want me to believe you! Go away! Otherwise, I'll call the police!" I resolutely took my cell phone out of my pocket. "After all, you say you're a werewolf, but I'm sorry, I don't see any wolf here! Once again, either you leave or I call the police! I don't..."

Before I could finish, Daniel smirked, rolled his eyes, and then... His eyes glowed again... His body began to transform rapidly, covered in sleek black fur. Before I knew it, a big black wolf was standing in front of me. A golden belt glittered on its belly. The man who'd told me the mystical stories about Adamantha the other day, his eyes were only a vivid violet.

I cried out in surprise. The wolf came right up to me and nuzzled into my hand. I didn't dare lift my palm and put it on the wolf's face. He seemed to like it. He closed his eyes and rubbed his muzzle against my palm.

"The police don't seem to help here," I said confusedly, "more like a stray animal rescue..."

Hearing this phrase, the wolf abruptly opened his eyes. The fur on the back of his neck stood on end, he growled softly.

"Okay, okay… I was kidding. I'm not…"

"Lacey! Where did you get that dog?"

We turned our heads together with the wolf at the sound of the man's voice. It made me want to fall to the ground. Henry was standing on the threshold of the living room, staring intently at me and at Daniel as the wolf. That would have been okay, except Henry was wearing nothing but a big towel carelessly wrapped around his thighs.

"Damn it, Lacey! What's wrong with his eyes?"

CHAPTER 10

"Let's Meet."
D.

A guy, wrapped in a towel, stood in the doorway, looking at us frightened. Apparently she doesn't live alone... I think I got the answer to my question... Yeah, well... It's not going to be easy, that's for sure... The story picks up steam.

"Lacey!" the guy continued hysterically. "Where did you get that weird dog?"

He called me a dog again. For the second time in the last two minutes. My patience was running out. I hated it when we werewolves were compared to dogs. Truly, we had nothing in common with those animals. I couldn't help myself, so I leaned forward a little and growled.

The boy jerked and took a step back. Yeah... Scared. That's right. Maybe from now on he'd get a better look to see who was in front of him.

Lacey must have thought I was going to attack her boyfriend, because she tried to stop me by grabbing the back of my neck. Her touch made me feel hot, and my veins felt like an electric current.

"Dan, don't... That's not what Henry meant."

It was as if she sensed the exact words that got me.

"Um... Henry. Why don't you get dressed... for starters... And then we'll talk... I'll tell you about Daniel, and you tell me how it was that you ended up in my house. Okay?"

"Daniel?" Henry was in no hurry to leave. "Is that his name?" He nodded in my direction. "That's a bit of an odd name for a dog..."

I growled quietly again.

"Henry... Please... Get dressed and come back," Lacey tried again to prevent a scandal.

With a shrug, Henry disappeared from view. Well, the first part of the play was over. More surprise awaits the guy when he returns.

Mentally, I grinned, slowly closed my eyes, and took a deep breath.

"Hey, hey... What are you doing?" exclaimed Lacey, frightened.

But it was too late. I was already standing in front of her as a human.

"How did you... How do you do that? Why you?"

Lacey looked at me and then at the living room door, where Henry had disappeared a moment ago.

"Why did you do those things of yours! How am I going to explain it to him now?"

I only grinned. I was beginning to be amused by the whole situation. You might even say I was getting a little high on the fact that I had put Lacey and her friend in a stupor. This was where my wolf nature kicked in. I could only anticipate the look on Henry's face when he returned. He doesn't know it yet, but... He didn't stand a chance with Lacey. If she was my true mate, Henry would definitely have to step aside. I don't think he'll be able to compete with me...

Continuing to smile, I looked at Lacey again. She was looking at me with eyes full of rage. Her hair was disheveled, and her chest was heaving with frequent sighs. The sight of her drew me in even more. I'd only known her for a day, but I was drawn to her like I'd known her for a hundred years. I wondered what would happen next. This attraction would become more and more difficult to control. When a werewolf meets his true mate, he loses those powers... Until they reunite... Otherwise... What happens then, I didn't even want to think about it... It was too sad a prospect... And I certainly wasn't ready to go through with it. So I would do anything to get me and Lacey back together. But later on... When the world wasn't threatened by Greif Volturis...

I took a step toward Lacey. There was a look of consternation in her eyes, but she didn't show it, and stayed where she was. Great. I stepped toward Lacey. She's not a shy one...

"Let's tell him the truth," I said. "Why hide anything? After all, we live in Adamantha... Anything can happen here..."

Lacey opened her mouth to contradict me once again, but didn't have time. There was a knock on the door somewhere, and footsteps. Henry came back into the room, already dressed. The boy did not fail to live up to my expectations.

"Lacey? Who's that?"

"Henry, I'll explain it all to you now, it's—"

"Daniel." I interrupted the girl, taking the initiative. "The same wolf you called a dog a few minutes ago..."

"What?" Henry darted his eyes at me. "Lacey, what's going on here? First the dog, then this guy... I don't understand anything... It's just..." Henry looked at me again. In his eyes, it was like a glimmer of a 'come on' hunch. "Is that really what I thought it was? It can't be! Are you a werewolf?"

CHAPTER 11

"Best Friends Forever."
L.

"Oh no! Wait, wait, wait... You what? Are you this? Are you really a werewolf?" Henry was getting carried away.

I just rolled my eyes. I was afraid of that reaction. With his love for all things mysterious... Henry was very fond of Adamantha's history, and he believed that all the references to the supernatural were true. He believed that one day he would meet someone extraordinary. And lo and behold... Daniel gave him that opportunity. The werewolf probably thinks he scared my friend, but... He just needs a little time to himself. From being happy... That his wish finally came true.

Now Daniel's not getting off easy. Henry's not letting him go anywhere.

He really isn't. Clapping his hands enthusiastically, Henry ran around the living room, uttering short phrases with a gasp.

"Finally! Yes! Yes! I knew it... I knew it was all true! They... They exist! I'm... And you!"

He turned and jabbed his finger at me.

"And you didn't believe me! You laughed at me! There, you see how it is? It's true! They are!"

Daniel was still silent, only staring silently at Henry, who was whizzing around the room as if he'd been stung by a wasp.

"What's the matter with him?" Daniel asked me quietly, watching Henry.

"Um… He's just…" I smiled. "He's just glad to see you."

Daniel raised an eyebrow in surprise.

"Yes, yes," I responded to his look. "It's Henry… He just loves all things dark and supernatural. You just made his childhood dream come true…"

"Ahem… That's… Is he your boyfriend?" Daniel continued to be at a loss.

"Who? Henry?" I laughed. "No, of course… He's my friend… A little weird, but… the best."

I was suddenly silent. Maybe I shouldn't have been so reckless as to tell Daniel the truth. Who knows what the transformer man would get into his head? Maybe knowing I had a boyfriend would cool his fervor a little. But… It looked like it was too late to rectify the situation.

"God… This is unbelievable!" Henry still couldn't calm down.

He walked over to Daniel and touched his shoulder.

"No, well, you… Are you really a werewolf? Look, can you do that thing again?"

Daniel raised his eyebrows again in surprise.

"Well that… Transformation…"

97

"Turning," clarified Daniel. "I can."

I looked at the guy in surprise. What? What kind of favor is that for Henry?

Daniel looked back at me. Something gleamed in his eyes. My intuition told me it wasn't a good glimmer. Daniel was up to something... I sighed desperately. How 'lucky' am I... Being in the company of two men who weren't quite adequate... What could be better?

"Just tell me, Lacey, your friend, she's always like this... um...?"

"Nerd?" Henry expressed a hunch. "Oh, forget it." He patted Daniel on the shoulder. "She never believed any of this..."

I only opened my mouth in indignation. But I couldn't say anything. I could only watch in silence as the two of them abruptly became 'best friends forever'.

"Actually, I have a very important conversation to have with Lacey. But she flatly refuses to listen to me. Perhaps you can help me convince her...."

Henry threw an angry look in my direction and turned to Daniel.

"I'd love to! You just tell me what you need..."

CHAPTER 12

"Welcome to the Panic Room."
D.

At first I didn't take Henry seriously. His reenactment only amused me. But then I realized that Henry, with his enthusiasm and heightened loyalty to supernatural beings, could help me. A plan quickly emerged in my mind. I planned to use Henry as the leverage that would help me persuade Lacey to go to Swamphorse and take the place that was hers by descent. Thinking about it, I got a little discouraged... How, then, to solve the other question. She is my true mate... How can we be in different cities, apart from each other? It would be impossible. I can't... A werewolf without his true mate just loses everything from strength to self-control.

There has to be a way out. As I pondered the issues at hand, Henry announced that he was willing to help me talk to Lacey. Calling the girl a nuisance several times, he assured me that the conversation would take place at any cost. I just smiled silently. This Henry was a little strange, but completely harmless... His emotion and delight at seeing me were genuine. He was really happy to see me...

I guess Lacey was right. The guy really did get his wish today. Well, it wouldn't be very nice of me to do that. But right now, it seems to be the only way. The only human way to reach an understanding with Lacey.

Henry pulled me toward the exit of the living room, obviously thinking that talking in front of Lacey meaningless.

"Hey! Did anyone forget about me?"

I heard Lacey's indignant voice behind me. Henry and I turned around together. The girl was standing across from us, staring indignantly. It seemed as if a little more, and from her eyes would fall sparks on our heads. I couldn't hold back a smile. Angry, she attracted me even more. I could smell the faint scent of violets again. It was what helped me find Lacey. Ever since I'd realized she was my true mate, the smell of those flowers had haunted me. I tried to remember the story. If my memory serves me right, this is one of the peculiarities of when a werewolf finds his mate. The smell. In this case, the smell of flowers. For each mate it is singular and unique. Especially so that you can easily find each other, relying on your senses.

"You figured it all out so quickly!" Lacey continued frantically. "But I have a number of questions for you! To you." She poked her finger at me. "You think you impressed me with your magic stuff and now I'm going to fall at your feet?"

I grinned. I don't need to tell you that I meant those words in a very different way. I didn't suffer from a lack of imagination, and my mind quickly painted a not-so-chaste picture in my mind.

And Lacey went on talking, unaware of what was going on in my head.

"So that's it! You were wrong! I won't look at you as a werewolf, and my warning still stands! Go away, or I'll call the police…"

"Lace." Henry tried to stop his friend. "But because…"

"And you!" Lacey immediately shifted her attention to Henry. "Don't you dare say anything! First of all, what are you doing here! When I called you, you said you had business!"

"I had a change of plans, you said you weren't feeling well, so I thought I'd surprise you by coming," Henry replied, "and it turns out you surprised me…"

"That's enough," shouted Lacey and she grabbed her head. "I'm sick of both of you! Go away! Both of you! I don't want to see you! You got along very well! So go save the world together, fight universal evil, and whatever else werewolves do! I don't…"

Lacey didn't get a chance to finish. The next second there was a deafening sound of shattering glass in the room. Shards of broken window shattered everywhere. A dark whirlwind swept across the room, knocking her off her feet. Lacey screamed, and Henry cringed against the wall, his eyes wide with frank horror. The Shadow worked on the effect of surprise. A powerful rush of air knocked me off my feet and tossed me aside. In the next second, it flew toward Lacey. Once again a gust of wind blew through, and the Shadow tossed Lacey aside. The girl's back hit the wall. With a low groan, Lacey slowly slid down the wall. The Shadow leaned ominously over her. I didn't hesitate for a second. I wouldn't let the Shadow hurt Lacey anyway, because she was a guardian. But now. It all intensified. Now this act of the Shadow had taken on a personal coloring for me. I was already flying toward the Shadow as a wolf. I only jumped up and released my claws to take out the next of Greif's henchmen. But the Shadow was beginning to take on human empathics. It extended its long black arm and deftly beat back my blow. Gosh, the bastard was much stronger than the ones I'd met the day before in Blackbrow wood. It looked like Greif Volturis was very well prepared.

I flew almost all the way across the room from the Shadow's blow, but it didn't knock me off my feet. I wasn't going to give up. I roared menacingly, and then I charged at the Shadow again.

"Shh," the Shadow whistled, and stood in front of me, separating me from Lacey and Henry.

Out of the corner of my eye, Henry ran up to the girl and started to help her up. Lacey seemed to come to her senses. I breathed a sigh of relief.

"Wolf." The Shadow kept whistling. "You can't s-s-stop it… You can't s-s-save her… His majesty is already here… Darkness will descend on Adamantha… This is his message to you. You can't save her. You will destroy each other and the world…"

With a whistle, the Shadow transformed back into a dark blob and flew out the broken window. There was a ringing silence. Even Quetown seemed to have stopped its busy nightlife. It was so quiet all around. Faster than lightning, I turned back into a human and rushed toward Lacey.

"Lacey." I landed beside her. Henry was supporting her by the shoulders. The guy's eyes never stopped looking frightened. "How are you?"

"I'm…" Lacey's voice sounded hoarse. "Like I was thrown into a wall by some dark something." Lacey sighed noisily and made an attempt to get up.

"Hey," Henry held her up. "Take your time. Are you sure you're okay? Does it hurt much?"

"It's bearable," answered Lacey heroically, "I take it you're not going to leave…"

She grinned crookedly. That must have been a good sign. If the irony came back to her, it meant she'd be on the mend soon. But I was scared out of my wits.

"Now you understand." I put my arm around her shoulders and peered into her eyes. "Why you have to go to Swamphorse? It's already started. Greif has opened a hunt for you…"

"Ahem… Dan?" stretched out Henry. "What do you mean? Is that what you wanted to talk to me about?"

"Yeah," I sighed, "Exactly. Lacey needs to go to Swamphorse right away."

"But why?" Henry continued to be perplexed.

"Because your friend is a witch…"

CHAPTER 13

"I'm with you."
L.

"A witch!" interjected Henry and stared at me. "What do you mean, a witch?"

"Literally," sighed Daniel. "Your friend is from an ancient family of witches who lived in Swamphorse. Their main purpose was to guard one of the portals, to prevent the Dark Forces from breaking through to our world."

Henry turned to me.

"Is that true, Lace? But why didn't you tell me anything?"

"Because I just found out about it myself today." I leaned my head back against the wall. "But honestly, I still have my doubts about his adequacy." I nodded at Daniel.

The guy just grinned again. He didn't seem to have enough of my words. He'd come here for a purpose, and he would get it at any cost. His eyes glinted the familiar violet color.

"Look, can you stop doing that? I'm a little uncomfortable…"

"What do you mean?" wondered Daniel.

"I think, she means your eyes," Henry clarified. "They're glowing now... Blue light..."

"Violet light..."

Henry and I said the last words together and looked at each other sharply. Of course, I wasn't as talented as Henry, and I couldn't tell the color Dark Moon from plain gray. But I certainly knew the difference between violet and blue.

"Hey, Lace, are you sure you're okay? What kind of violet is that?"

I looked at Daniel.

"Do you have anything to say? Which one of us is going crazy?"

Daniel smiled.

"Actually," he began to say, "the hallmark of werewolf-empathics has always been bright blue eyes..."

"Yep!" Henry exclaimed too loudly. It made me flinch. "I said blue! Lacey, should we call a doctor?"

"Is it really that bad?" I squinted at Daniel.

"They really are blue, but... The fact that you see them differently is... It's like a sign of how supernatural beings distinguish each other. Anyway, that just proves my point. You really are a guardian..."

"But then why is she... nothing happens to her? Why is she normal?" Henry persisted.

I glared at him. Yeah, sometimes a sense of tact gets away from Henry.

"Thank you, dear friend." I grinned skeptically. "I've never had anyone pay me such exquisite compliments...

But by the way, I'm curious about that, too. What's wrong with me? Apparently, I'm supposed to walk through the woods in a black hoodie collecting plants and drying frogs."

"You have a very stereotypical idea of what a witch is," smiled Daniel.

"Perhaps… But where are all those superpowers? Until today, I didn't even think that was even possible…"

"It's most likely a muted power… I think that one of your predecessors, how should I put it… sealed your powers? Hoping that it might keep you from encountering the Dark powers. What we saw today means only one thing: Greif knows who you are. Now he will try any way he can to destroy you. This will help him break the triangle's circuit and open the portals. That's why you need to get to Swamphorse as soon as possible. The portal's power will protect you from Greif, and you, in turn, will be able to protect the circuit from breaking… This Shadow." Daniel glanced around at the mess the dark creature had left behind. "Is just the beginning. Greif won't give up trying to take you down…"

Daniel fell silent, and Henry and I tried to come to our senses, too. It all seemed absurd and unreal.

"Lace." Henry and I seemed to be thinking the same thing. "I know it sounds unbelievable, but… I think Dan's right. I don't know what's wrong with your powers, but if it's about your life, then… Maybe it really is better to leave. It's just, what we saw today…"

Henry stopped talking. I didn't know what to say, either. Really, it was all kind of surreal, but... Maybe Daniel was right. And it's not safe here? What if that dark something wanted to come back? After all, Daniel might not be around... It was weird, but... Somehow I was glad he was here at this moment.

Ignoring the boys' help, I got up slowly. Somehow we'd spent the last few minutes talking in the position in which the Shadow has left us.

"It's all so complicated..."

I walked to the broken window and looked out at the city at night.

"You may be right, but... I've only known you for one day. You come to me and tell me this incredible story... I can't say I don't believe you. After all, we live in Adamantha, anything is possible here, but... I've lived my life without knowing anything... And now what? Do I have to leave everything and go to the middle of nowhere? Alone?"

Daniel got up from his seat and walked toward me. His eyes still twinkled slightly. He took my hand. The warmth of his wide palm sent a pleasant wave through my body.

"Well, actually, no... No one's going to let you go in there alone. That's for one thing. And second of all... I'll be there for you. I'll be with you."

CHAPTER 14

"We Leave at Dawn."
D.

I could feel her sadness and despair. In some ways, even literally. Werewolves were pretty good at reading emotions. And if they were a true mates, they could sense how their partner was feeling. Lacey was in a mixed bag of feelings, fear peeking through the sadness and confusion. It wasn't a bad thing that fear wasn't the main feeling. But… I tried to reassure her. I don't know if I succeeded or not… Was my promise to be with her a comfort to her? I even made up a story about the color of my eyes, so as not to give her too much to worry about. I told her it was how she distinguished the supernatural, but… The answer was actually different. She saw my eyes differently because we were meant to be together. That's exactly why. But how could I begin to tell her about the true mates when she had just found out who she really was? All I could do now really was be there for her, as I had promised…

Lacey looked out the window a little more.

"Well." It was as if she had made some big decision. "If you say it's for the best... Okay... let's go to Swamphorse... If that Greif wants me that badly, let him pick me up there. Not here... Without destroying my town and the lives of my loved ones..."

"That's very noble of you, of course." I grinned. "But don't think anyone will give you to him so easily."

"When do we go?" Lacey ignored my statement.

"At dawn, I think. I need to make some calls to get us secured a corridor to Swamphorse. If the Shadows made it to Quetown, we may not have a very pleasant surprise waiting for us on the road."

"At dawn... So fast... But... I won't even have time to finish my business... I have to call Peter, decide with the club and—"

"Lace," Henry interrupted me, "that's the last thing you should be thinking about right now. I'll talk to Peter myself tomorrow. I think he'll understand."

"Right. Peter will definitely understand," I said.

"How do you know?" wondered Lacey. "Oh, yeah, because he said you two were old friends... Wait! Peter, him? Also? One of those?"

Lacey's face stretched at such an assumption. I hastened to reassure her.

"No... Not really."

"You mean?"

"Peter's father was a werewolf. His mother was human. Somehow, Peter didn't inherit his father's genes."

"No way," Henry exclaimed, "all those years working with him… I wish he'd said something about it…"

"Not that we're hiding much… But no one wants to shout openly about their true nature. That's why." Daniel shrugged. "That's why it happened."

"What else don't I know?" asked Lacey ironically, "what other secrets are on the agenda?"

I wondered. Maybe I should have told her. Wouldn't I undermine her trust in me? Or should I wait for the right moment? Should I wait for her to sort out her powers? Maybe then it would be easier?

Lacey interpreted my silence in her own way.

"Okay. Peter's been dealt with. But this." She waved her hand at the broken window. "I can't leave my apartment like this."

"Lace, I'll solve it. I'll call a handyman tomorrow, he'll fix it."

Lacey squinted.

"I get the feeling you want to get rid of me sooner so you can use my apartment…"

"And I get the feeling that you're procrastinating because you don't want to leave. And I understand you, but it's about your life right now… So don't be silly!"

Lacey frowned. I liked watching the way these two talked to each other.

"All right." Lacey stretched out uncertainly. "But… Right! How could I forget! How could they?" she exclaimed and ran to the balcony. I looked questioningly at Henry. The guy just shrugged his shoulders. We ran out after Lacey.

"How am I going to leave them?"

There was a small table on the balcony with a few flower pots on it. They were violets. The little violet flowers were blooming so exuberantly that it was impossible to see the tabletop at a glance.

"Violets?" I smiled. "You're also a florist?"

"No. It's from my childhood... When we lived in the old house... with my parents, we had a little flowerbed... Those violets are from there... I used to love to fiddle with them... After my parents died, I took them from there... They remind me of them... of a past life..."

"Well... If these flowers are so important to you, I guess it won't be a problem if we take them with us..."

"Really?" Lacey's eyes lit up.

Her reaction had a strange effect on me. When she was happy, it made me feel good, too. Which reassured me once again that I wasn't wrong. Lacey really was my true mate. The words of the Prophecy came to mind, and they ruled it all out, me and her. But... I brushed those thoughts aside. I didn't want to think about it now. There had to be a solution. I would find it, no matter what it cost me... With every minute I spent with her, I knew that I wouldn't let her go. We would be together, even if the world collapsed...

We agreed to leave at dawn. Lacey was very tired from the day, so Henry and I sent her to bed, reasoning that she needed to rest before the road. She resisted, but not for long. She frowned a little, but she wandered off to her room.

Henry and I were left alone in the living room. While we tried to clean up a bit, I repeated the whole story again to Henry from the beginning. The boy listened with his mouth open. He really seemed to think it was the best day of his life. There was a childlike delight in his eyes. After making me promise to keep an eye on Lacey and bring her back to Quetown, Henry drifted off to bed, too.

I glanced at my watch. It was one o'clock in the morning. The fun must be in full swing at the Lunar Eclipse. I didn't think Peter was asleep. I'd have to warn him. I didn't know exactly what Henry would tell him, so I decided to prepare my friend. Peter didn't answer the phone for a long time. A feeling of anxiety began to creep up on me. But finally, my friend answered.

"Hello?" Peter's voice sounded strangely strained.

I was a little surprised.

"Did I wake you up?"

"No. I'm working. What did you want?"

I took the phone off my ear and looked at the phone. I certainly didn't get the wrong number.

"Are you okay?"

"Yeah," Peter sighed, "just a lot of work. How are you?"

"I don't even know how to say this… I'm at Lacey's right now… It's a little worse than we thought…"

"What happened?" Peter perked up.

"A Shadow broke into her house. And delivered a message from Greif. He made it clear that he had opened a hunt for Lacey…"

"Really? And what did you do?"

"It didn't manage to hurt her, of course, but… You do realize how dangerous that is, don't you? Anyway, Lacey and I are going to Swamphorse in the morning…"

There was silence on the phone. I looked at the screen again.

"Pete? Are you there?"

"Yeah. Yeah. I think you made the right decision. Lacey needs to get out of here. Okay, Dan, I have to go. Keep me posted."

Without waiting for my answer, Peter hung up. Puzzled, I put the phone away. What was wrong with him? He was talking strangely… Nothing bad had happened, I hope?

The time before dawn flew by almost imperceptibly. I spent it thinking about everything. What would we do with Lacey at Swamphorse? How would I tell her the truth? Would we make it? Was the circuit so broken that it was too late to fix it?

CHAPTER 15

"Native Lands."
L.

When I opened my eyes, it was already light outside. But the new day brought no relief. I looked at the large suitcase in the corner of the room. Despite my condition, I still decided to pack from the evening. I kept feeling like I was in a play of the absurd. It all seemed unreal. If someone had told me a couple of days ago that I would be leaving at dawn in the company of a werewolf... Well... I don't know what I would have said to that person... I guess I'd ask if he'd had too much to drink. And now... I walked out of my bedroom and into the living room. Daniel was standing by the broken window, looking off into the distance.

"Didn't you go to bed at all?" I walked closer to him and looked out the window. The city was still asleep, even though the scarlet streak of dawn was already lit up in the sky.

"Couldn't sleep... Yes, and we don't need much time to rest. How are you?"

"If I say okay, it would be a lie," I hummed. "I'm confused... I don't know what awaits me... My old life is ruined... Hmm... Somehow..."

"Look, you may not believe me, of course, but I promise you that I will do everything I can to help you... and save you."

"Thank you." I smiled sadly and looked at Daniel. His eyes had already responded with such familiar violet sparks. Something in my chest gave me a little tingle. I hoped he wouldn't have to save me from himself...

It was almost dawn when we got out of the driveway. I stopped before I took a step. Daniel stopped beside me.

"Ready?"

"I don't know," I answered quietly. And it was true. The unknown waited ahead. Could I be ready for it?

"Come on." Daniel nodded toward his car and held out his hand to me. I looked at his palm. After thinking for a while, I took his hand. Well, I hope I'm making the right choice now... Which would not only save my life, but also save humanity...

***

We walked halfway there in silence. I stared at the familiar scenery outside the window, which remained behind us. Would I be able to go back to Quetown again? When? Would I be able to do what Daniel was talking about? What kind of witch would I be? How could I awaken these powers within me? Suddenly it hit me. I wondered if my mother knew about this. I guess she did... According to Daniel, it's all hereditary... So they really didn't want me to go through all this... How is that... When am I going to get used to all this? I still haven't fully accepted that this story is about me. I didn't get into the movie or the book... It's all real. This is my life... My new life...

"Why do you dance?" Daniel broke the silence. I didn't immediately understand what he meant. He saw my questioning expression, so he hurried to clarify. "You dance at the club... Why? You're the owner of the club... It's so unusual..."

I smiled...

"It's my past... I went to choreography college... I always liked to dance... I wanted a career in dance..."

"What went wrong?"

"I wrote the script, but life made adjustments to it... My parents were in a car accident... It got me down. I fell out of reality... I dropped out of school... I never got back... It happened on the eve of the concert... I was waiting for them, but... they never came... I went on stage knowing they weren't here, but I thought they were just late..."

I fell silent. It was always hard for me to remember... Even though so many years had passed, the wound was still open...

"What happened next?" asked Daniel quietly.

"The teacher came up to me after the concert and told me that my parents crashed in an accident... And then... then darkness came... I don't remember how I lived all that time. And if it wasn't for Henry... I don't know if I'd be sitting here with you now..."

I fell silent. Remembering that day was still hard, despite the fact that many years had passed. But, oddly enough, I was relieved to tell Daniel about it. It was as if all this had been accumulating in me for such a long time and now I let my grief out...

Further we did not touch upon such sensitive topics. Daniel told me about himself and his family. And some more Blackbrow history. It was interesting to listen to. for a moment it even seemed to me that we, like old friends, were going somewhere to rest. Certainly, our trip did not have such a terrible and global goal ...

Travel time flew by. I did not have time to look back, as we were already driving along the country road of one of the streets of Swamphorse.

"Do you know anything here?" Daniel asked as he circled a large puddle.

I looked around.

"No. I don't know this place at all. Although... Mom once mentioned a grandmother who did not live with us, but... It was a short conversation... She did not return to him again."

Finally, we pulled up to a small red-brick house. Daniel stopped the car.

"Are we there?" I asked, eyeing the area.

"Yes," answered Daniel, unbuckling his belt.

He opened the doors and got out of the car. I followed his example.

"Listen." The thought occurred to me. "How are we going to get in? We don't have keys."

But Daniel didn't seem to see the problem. He walked silently around the car, pulled his backpack and my suitcase out of the trunk.

"Let's go." He nodded at the iron gate and walked confidently toward the house, carrying our things.

Uncomprehending, I followed him. I guess a sense of self-confidence was inherent in all supernatural beings. Keeping his casual expression, Daniel strode up the battered stone path to the porch. Climbing the steps, Daniel walked to the door and quickly looked back. Then he grasped the doorknob.

"Hey! Are you going to break it in?"

"Do you have keys?"

"No... Although now I think I should have looked for them at home. They're probably somewhere in my mom's things."

"Clever thought... Well, let's use the key next time... We don't have much time to go back to Quetown right now."

"Very funny." I rolled my eyes.

Daniel smiled and continued to manipulate the door. He squeezed the doorknob hard. There was a slight cracking sound. Daniel's eyes gleamed with violet light again. After a second, he swung the door open.

"It's open."

We stepped into the half-dark porch of the house. The dark, dense curtains kept the sunlight out altogether. I looked around. A small couch in the corner, a closet nearby, a table, and a few chairs. The veranda reminded me of a horror movie setting. Everything was dilapidated and abandoned. Cobwebs dangled everywhere, and the surfaces were strewn with a thick layer of dust. A sense of despondency overtook me. I suddenly wanted to burst into tears.

I guess what was going on only caught up with me now.

"Hey, are you okay?" Daniel turned to me.

"I… Say, are you going to leave me here? Will you leave? And I'll stay in this weird house?"

I felt like a little helpless child. I froze, waiting for his answer.

Daniel looked at me carefully and smiled slightly. He took a few steps in my direction. There was hardly any space between us.

"I told you the day before, I'm not leaving you. I'm not leaving here until we get this all sorted out. Stop thinking about it. We'll get through this. You have no idea how strong you are. We just need to find a way to unleash your powers. And we will. Very soon. Okay?"

I just nodded. Definitely, Daniel's presence was affecting me strangely. I felt comfortable around him, despite the gravity of the situation. And it was scary to think that at some point he might not be there.

"Okay, well, I suggest we look for something like a store, and then we'll look around the house. How do you feel about that?"

Daniel took the situation into his own hands. And rightly so. I wasn't much use to him.

We walked for a long time down the spacious street. Strangely, Swamphorse seemed empty. As we walked, we didn't see a single person. The town was somehow suspiciously quiet.

Finally, some sounds were heard somewhere in the distance. Thinking there was some sort of central square, Daniel and I walked in that direction.

Our senses were right. We were indeed in the center of Swamphorse. Life was in full swing here. People were scurrying back and forth, and there were little bins of merchandise everywhere. There were even a few cafes with summer terraces. In general, Swamphorse looked like a medieval town. It seemed that civilization had not fully reached here. We oriented ourselves by the signs and entered one of the pavilions, assuming that here we could get some food and water. There was almost no one in the store. Only a saleswoman was talking to some nice grandmother.

When the women saw us, they were silent and started looking at us.

"Good afternoon." Daniel broke the awkward silence.

"Hello," replied the saleswoman warily. Her companion only nodded her head silently. Remaining nonchalant, Daniel made his way inside the rows. I lingered at the counter with the postcards. There were many pictures of Swamphorse in different angles. Looking at the pictures, I was once again convinced that Swamphorse was from the Middle Ages...

"Have you travelled far to get to us?" I shuddered as I heard a voice behind me.

I turned around. The women were watching me with interest, waiting for an answer.

"From Quetown." I tried to be friendly and smiled.

"Are you here to see someone?"

I hesitated, not knowing what to answer. These women seemed to be of the cohort of local gossipy women. And I didn't really want me and Daniel to be the object of everyone's attention.

"Yes," I answered uncertainly. I wouldn't go into too much detail. Would a simple affirmative answer be enough for them?

"Wait a minute." The older woman squinted at me. "Alia, does she remind you of anyone?"

The saleswoman focused her gaze on me, too.

"Lynette, I don't know what you mean? Don't mind me." Alia turned to me. "Lynette, our long-time resident, she thinks she knows everyone and everything here."

"No, she doesn't." Lynette stood her ground. "She certainly reminds me of someone. A very familiar face..."

Lynette continued to study my face. It got awkward.

"You must be mistaken." I smiled. "This is our first time here. I don't think we've ever met."

"I'm not saying I've seen you before," Lynette snorted, "you just remind me of someone... Exactly! I remember! You're Stefania's granddaughter, aren't you?"

Lynette looked at me with a look of triumph.

"Who? I don't…"

"Exactly." I suddenly felt someone's hand on my waist. In some incomprehensible way, Daniel was beside me. While I was chatting with Alia and Lynette, he'd already had time to run through the store and fill the basket.

"What are you…" I tried to be indignant, but Daniel just hugged me tighter, as if to warn me not to say too much.

"That's right. Lacey is Stefania's granddaughter. Her grandmother left her the house as a legacy. We finally managed to get away to look at it…"

"I told you!" exclaimed Lynette. "She looks just like Stefania, just the same face! You can't fool me! Finally, there will be life in this house again. I hope you'll stick around for a while. It's so sad to walk past her empty house."

The mention of my grandmother's name, coupled with the definition of kinship, seemed to serve as a password. The caution disappeared. Lynette, and then Alia, became lusciously friendly. Daniel and I were barely able to escape the company of these two women. They had time to tell us a brief history of Stefania's life and were genuinely pleased with our happiness. For some reason they thought that Daniel and I were a couple. In case someone else looked at me and remembered my grandmother. I guess she was pretty famous around here…

"How did you know that my grandmother's name was Stefania?" I asked Daniel when we were back on the deserted street from which we had begun our journey.

"I used to come here before I came to Quetown. Outside the house, I met a woman. About the same as Lynette, she interrogated me about who I was and who I was looking for."

"It's so strange... I don't even know my grandmother's name... I don't know anything about her at all... And about myself..."

"I think your house holds a lot of answers... We'll have something to do in the near future."

I had no choice but to agree with Daniel. Well, let's begin this fascinating quest...

CHAPTER 16

"Secrets of the Old House."
D.

Lacey's grandmother's house really did hold a lot of interesting things. All we had to do was open the dark curtains that hung from each window. There were old books scattered everywhere, and in the kitchen we found a lot of old cookware... Everything was in its place, from clothes to other household items. It was as if time itself had frozen the house.

I have to admit, I was a little confused. Yes, I could easily identify Lacey as my true mate, but... I had absolutely no idea how exactly we were supposed to awaken her powers. In theory, only the witch who'd put it there could lift the muffler, but... Stefania and Lacey's mother were dead... we had to find another way. I didn't have a clue. To avoid unnerving Lacey, I decided to help her look around the house. That seemed to calm her down a bit. She stopped being so tense. I decided I was going to call my father tonight; he must know something for sure.

"What made that Lynette think I looked like her?"

Lacey had already made it to another room. I went at the sound of her voice. It seemed to be Stefania's bedroom. I don't know why I thought that... Something told me. Lacey was standing with her back to me, holding some old picture in her hands.

"Here, look, do we look alike?"

The girl held out the photo to me. I took the picture in my hands and looked at the image. I felt my eyebrows go up in surprise. The picture was of a middle-aged woman. Wearing a wide-brimmed hat and holding a bouquet of wild flowers.

Even though the photo was old, and its quality left a lot to be desired, it wasn't hard for me to recognize the woman. She was the one who had spoken to me when I first came to Swamphorse! But... Suddenly everything became clear to me... I was wrong. I thought the chill that ran between us was a harbinger of her imminent death, but... What it really meant was that she was a witch.

"Dan, what's wrong with you? Is something wrong?" Lacey looked at me worriedly.

"No, no, it's okay, it's just... Yeah, you and her really don't look much alike... except for the eyes... A little bit..."

For now, I decided not to tell Lacey that I saw her grandmother. I think she's had enough of the shock for now.

Before we knew it, it was evening. We managed to get the house more or less in order. Since the electricity there was no Stefania in the house, there was nothing to count on such benefits of civilization as a microwave or stove. We decided to organize dinner in the barbecue style.

Lacey went to prepare the groceries and find dishes, while I took care of the wood and the fire. It was not difficult for me to chop wood and light a fire. Lacey hasn't left yet. I decided not to rush her and seize the moment. I urgently needed to talk to my father. The question of the awakening of Lacey's powers remained open…

My father and I discussed the whole situation. I was relieved to hear that Blackbrow was more or less quiet.

"Father, I don't know what to do with Lacey? How can she awaken her powers? Who can break this spell?"

"Dan, it's not your concern any more. You should have taken her to Swamphorse. The power of the portal will do the rest."

"But…"

"Dan, you're needed here. Now all the guardians are in place. We need to concentrate our forces here."

"Dad, I can't go back… Without Lacey… I can't leave her alone."

"What? Dan, what are you talking about? You know what… Damn it! Just don't tell me that."

I knew what my father meant. And his guesses were correct.

"Dan, but how is that? How could this happen? She promised that this would not happen! She…"

My father fell silent in mid-sentence. On the contrary, I was concerned.

"I don't understand… What do you mean?"

My father was silent. And I felt that he was hiding something important from me.

"What's going on? Explain to me!"

He just sighed loudly.

"The fact that Lacey will become your true mate has been known for a long time. I clearly remember how we came to visit them in Swamphorse... We were friends... And you... You and Lacey... We understood where everything was going, but..."

"But what? What can be here «but»?" I started to run out of air. I didn't expect such betrayal...

"Dan, understand... You're a werewolf, she's a guardian... You can't be together."

"But why?"

"You are different... Too much... Your union will upset the entire balance that has been maintained in Adamantha for thousands of years... You are the hereditary guardian, Lacey too... You should be each near your portal... Your love is doomed."

"Why doesn't she remember me? Do I remember her?"

"Stefania took her memories... And yours too... This shouldn't have happened... You shouldn't have met."

"But we met! And this can't be changed! And you know what? I won't give up on her! I don't give a damn about all these prophecies of yours! Let the world shatter into smithereens. But I won't back down! But you know what makes me feel the worst right now?"

"I know, son, I know... I couldn't tell you... You would have rushed to the search at that very moment... I was afraid of losing you... And Stefania her granddaughter..."

"You know, not in vain." I smiled sarcastically. "Not in vain I was afraid... I can't forgive you for this, I..."

I did not have time to finish, because I suddenly heard a sharp cry from Lacey. Ignoring my father's exclamations on the phone, I rushed into the house. Lacey lay on the floor, in the middle of the room. Her hand was bloodied, something flashed under it. I ran closer. Mirror. Her hand rested on a small round mirror. I glanced briefly at my reflection. A huge black wolf was looking at me from the other side. A huge black wolf with violet eyes...

CHAPTER 17

"Stefania."
L.

I found myself back in that strange misty forest. Only now I saw a dark silhouette in the distance. Of course, the first thing I thought about was that I needed to get to this silhouette.

I resolutely took a few steps across the wet grass. There was a crunch of branches nearby. I winced and turned around. A black wolf approached me. The wolf flashed his violet eyes and rested his muzzle on my hand. Daniel. Of course it was him... There are no more wolves like him. I recognize him among thousands of others...

We slowly moved forward. The silhouette was getting closer. We did not walk quietly, small branches crunched under our feet every now and then. But the silhouette was in no hurry to address. It was like he didn't hear us at all. It was only when Daniel and I got really close that he froze and straightened abruptly.

"At last you have come, my child."

Surprisingly, the silhouette spoke in a soft, female voice. But somehow it made me feel even more afraid. As if Daniel sensed my fear, he came closer and pressed himself against me.

"Is the wolf here, too?"

Forgetting that the woman couldn't see me, I nodded. After standing with her back to us for a few more seconds, the woman took off her hood and slowly turned around. I groaned. Stefania was standing in front of me. I'd been looking at her picture just a few hours ago, and I'd been thinking that we didn't look anything alike. And now, there she was, standing in front of me in person.

"Well hello." She looked at Daniel. "Again."

I shifted my gaze from Stefania to Daniel. But the wolf's ears perked up. The fur on his scruff stood up, and his eyes glowed even brighter.

"Yes, you're here for a reason. Both of you. It's about time."

"Time for what?" I didn't understand.

"The confrontation between light and dark has already begun... And only you can help the light win..."

"But... Look... Dan, he's a werewolf and everything, but I... What can I do?"

Stefania grinned.

"Why so formal? I'm your grandmother, after all, child."

"Yeah, I mean... Sorry... But... I've never seen you..."

"Yes." Stefania stretched out and looked up, where the treetops were closing in on each other, creating the feeling of a dome "your mother wanted it that way... she refused to take the gift from me... and forbade me to give it to you... But your inner power is so powerful that you were able to break the muffling..."

"What do you mean, break it? But I don't know how to do anything... And I don't know..."

"It only seems that way to you, child... Your power burst forth, bypassing all inhibitions. Now you two must go to the stone..."

"But... Daniel said I should be here in Swamphorse, guarding the portal..."

"Too late... They're on their way... There will be a battle tonight... You need to leave for the stone... There your forces will unite... Otherwise..."

"Otherwise what?" I exclaimed impatiently. "What will happen?"

"The shadow will consume you... You must go to the stone... You are one... When the blood falls on the stone, there will be light..."

"What? But I don't... I don't understand... What does that mean? And I, my powers, this..."

"You've already opened them, child... The blood has already fallen on the glass... Now, the stone..."

"I don't understand..."

Suddenly a strong wind blew in. Huge trees bowed to the ground like boughs. Ominous Shadows began to surround us. But they didn't seem to be interested in me and Daniel. They brought all their power down on Stefania. I must have felt some kind of kinship in me, because I jerked toward Stefania. But Daniel wouldn't let me. He flashed his eyes at me, and stood between me and Stefania, who was being overpowered by the Shadows.

"You are one… The blood that fell on the stone will shed light… You are one…"

Stefania disappeared into the abyss of the Shadows, and her last phrase still rang in my head…

"Lacey… Lacey, wake up! Lacey!"

I opened my eyes. Right in front of me, I saw a sparkling violet color. Daniel was looking at me worriedly.

"What was that? Did you see that, too?"

"Yes," Daniel answered briefly and helped me up.

"But how? How did you end up there? You were a wolf…"

Daniel nodded.

"Apparently, your grandmother was a very powerful witch… And she wasn't too lazy to pass all her powers to you… How's your hand? Did you cut yourself?"

Daniel took my hand and looked at my palm. Just as he touched me lightly, something flashed before my eyes, like lightning. In that brief flash, I managed to see an image. A girl sitting beside a bed of purple flowers…

"Violets," I said when I realized what kind of flowers they were.

Another flash and the picture changed. Mom and Dad are sitting at a big table in the garden, and next to them are two men: an older man and the same age as Dad. The door of the house opened, and Stefania appeared on the threshold. She looked younger than in the picture and in that strange vision, but I recognized her…

I squeezed my eyes shut tightly and opened them sharply. The vision disappeared. I was standing in the kitchen of the cabin with Daniel again.

"Lacey, what's going on?"

"I... I don't know..." I looked at him. As soon as our eyes met, Daniel's eyes lit up brighter than usual, and I was thrown back into another vision.

The girl was still sitting by the flowerbed. A boy came up to her and sat down next to her. They looked at each other, smiling and talking about something. The scent of violets wafted around, and the boy's eyes shone... glowing violet...

I came to my senses again and looked at my palm in Daniel's hand. At that moment, something had happened. It was as if someone in my mind had torn away the black curtain. I was holding Daniel's hand, and I could see bits and pieces of my life flashing before my eyes, as if I were in an accelerated movie. No... Unbelievable... It couldn't be...

My subconscious movie was over. I looked at the werewolf again.

"You..." I exhaled.

"Lacey, are you okay? What's going on?"

"You." I continued to hold Daniel's hand and was shocked at what I was about to say. "Why do I feel like I... love you?"

CHAPTER 18

"I Think I Love You."
D.

When I heard her words, I froze in place. I only froze on the outside. Inside, I was in a hurricane. I felt like I was losing control. My blood was coursing through my veins at an incredible rate, my eyes must have glowed like you could see them in Quetown... I was on the verge of turning.

"What did you say?" I exhaled.

"The boy who came to play with me." The words poured out of Lacey in a torrent. "It was you... and those people, with my parents... Your father and probably my grandfather, too... We... We knew each other before... We used to see each other a lot... I always looked at your eyes... Violets... That's why I love them so much... Because they reminded me of your eyes..."

Lacey gasped and clamped her hand over her mouth. It was as if she couldn't believe what she was saying. It seems Stefania was right... I don't know how she managed to get me and Lacey into that mirror, but... Lacey really seemed to have awakened her powers. What's more, she started to remember her past life. Which to me was a huge plus. I was in her life. Dad wasn't lying. We were destined for each other.

"Jesus... They lied to us for so many years." Tears came to Lacey's eyes. "They knew we loved each other and still did it. We lived in darkness for so many years..."

I didn't know exactly what she saw in that moment, but her words were enough for me. Yes, it didn't bring back my memories, but... I felt it the first time I saw her. Even then I knew that she was mine, and that we would be together at any cost... Well, I guess I should thank Stefania...

Meanwhile, Lacey was no longer holding back. Large, clear tears poured from her eyes. I didn't think long. After all, I can do this legally now, can't I?

I walked over to Lacey and hugged her tightly. The girl's face was against my chest. Yes, she was crying, but in that moment I was the happiest on earth. I calmed her down, wiped away her tears, and never let her cry again. The most important thing is that now we will be together. No explanations, no misunderstandings, no silly spells...

"Shh, shh." I stroked her hair. The familiar scent of violets whirled in the air again. "But we're together now. I told you, I won't leave you alone."

She looked up at me with her tearful eyes.

"Really? You won't leave me? It was as if I had experienced the pain that had accumulated all these years, when I realized that I loved you, but I could not be there for you."

"No way! Now we're together until the very end! I don't care what they say! I won't forgive them for this! They took so many happy years away from me!"

I couldn't hold back any longer. I was so beckoned by her lips. I kissed her. Lacey hesitated a little, but she responded to my kiss, nonetheless.

But we didn't enjoy each other for long. The scary noise outside distracted our attention from each other. We ran out into the courtyard without talking. I froze at what I saw. There was impenetrable darkness outside. The wind was bending the tops of the trees mercilessly to the ground. Lightning flashed all around. It took me a second to realize that it wasn't just darkness. It was Shadows. There were many of them. So many…

"What's going on?" asked Lacey, frightened.

"I think we have company." I grinned. "But for some reason I don't feel like being hospitable at all…"

"Stone… Stefania said we have to go to the rock to be saved…"

"Right… Looks like we need to team up now… We need to go to Understone… Just…"

"What?"

A Shadow snuck between us. I grabbed Lacey's arm and pulled her toward the car. I almost pushed her inside and jogged into the driver's seat.

"I'll tell you about it on the way…"

CHAPTER 19

"Escaping."
L.

We got off to an abrupt start. I think one of the Shadows even threw itself under the car. Lightning flashed ahead, and it felt like we were driving into the middle of a storm. Daniel was pushing as hard as he could. I was beginning to worry that the car could be left without a bottom. We rushed on and on, but there were no fewer Shadows. The concentration seemed to get even higher. But in spite of that, we still managed to get out of Swamphorse. Except... Understone was very far away. We had a good chance of not getting there alive. Well... at least for me... Daniel had made it clear that Greif needed me, to put it mildly, in a certain state...

I suddenly thought of Mom and Dad. They knew about everything, but no one said a word about it... Were they protecting us? From whom? From what? Now to make us regret all the years we could have spent together...

"Dan." I remembered suddenly, thinking. "How do you know Stefania? She told you: 'Hello, again...' You... remember her?"

"No," replied Daniel, trying to keep the car steady. "I talked to my father the day before... He was just telling me about your grandmother taking our memories... I wanted to tell you about it, but... You beat me to it..."

"So you don't remember all that? What I told you?"

"No, I don't remember, but... When I first saw you... I don't need those memories any more... I already knew then who you were... And it wasn't the past. I looked at you and I knew you were my true mate... My senses confirmed that hunch... And when you told me about your eyes... Everything became clear in its entirety..."

"Meaning?"

"Werewolves have bright blue eyes. That..."

"I remember you talking about it, but you said it was part of a witch's magical powers."

"Not really. When a werewolf finds a true mate, I mean specifically a empath, he can find her by scent. According to ancient lore, it's the smell of different colors. In our case, it's violets. That is how I found your home and came to you. By the smell of violets. And when you told me how you see my eyes, it all came together, like two times two..."

"Look... Maybe they really did it because they had to." I squinted out the window. I don't know where we were, but there were far fewer Shadows. "Maybe this is all happening now because of us?"

"No!" exclaimed Daniel too sharply. When he saw that I flinched, he added in a softer tone, "Lacey, you said yourself that we lost a lot of time because of them! I don't care! Let the world fall on our heads now, but I won't give you up to anyone else! We'll be together, against all odds! I don't want to live without you for so long any more!"

Daniel squeezed my hand tightly, holding the steering wheel with his free hand. I wasn't adventurous, but I liked this plan. I realized that just a few hours ago, I didn't know anything at all about Daniel, and now... My feelings for him burned, and I knew I would follow him into fire and water... And jump into the abyss... It was a strange animal call. A call of passion and feeling and ownership.

"How far are we to Understone?"

"About ten hours. We'll be there by morning," sighed Daniel. "The main thing is to get there before Greif. He won't be able to stand up to the three of us. I've warned the special forces. They're on their way, too. I think we could use some support..."

We pulled onto an empty highway. There were no cars at all. The Shadows were gone, too. But I wasn't in a hurry to calm down. I really hoped it wasn't a moment of calm before the storm. The big, full moon lit up the road. I think it was quiet out there. I could even feel the ominous silence outside the car window, even though the engine was noisy. A motel loomed up ahead, beckoning with its neon sign. Daniel turned toward the building.

"Are we staying here?"

"We need to fill up the car and rest. We don't know what we'll face tomorrow. I have to be in shape to be able to protect you."

"So I'm kind of like a super powerful witch." I grinned. "You don't think I can stand up for myself?"

"I don't doubt that." Daniel squeezed my hand tighter. "But I'd feel safer if you stayed out of the open fight. Besides, I promised you I wouldn't leave you alone..."

We got the job done very quickly. We filled up the car and rented a room. It was a small cozy room on the second floor. We only had enough time to take a shower and make it to the bed, which, by the way, was a double. But, apparently, my fatigue did not focus on this. Or maybe I wanted it to... After all, I found out how I felt about Daniel. Wasn't he the one I was supposed to share this bed with?

When we finally settled down, I didn't hesitate to run my hand over his torso, lingering a little on his stomach. Daniel flinched, and I jerked my hand away.

"I'm sorry, I just..."

But he didn't let me finish, closing his mouth with a kiss. And then... We found ourselves in each other's arms and the little motel room was filled with passion, hot kisses, hands and feet entwined and moans of pleasure...

CHAPTER 20

"Help Me Remember."
D.

I woke up to a cool gust of wind. The white curtains fluttered in front of the open window. The sun was just beginning to rise over the horizon. I turned my head. Lacey was serenely asleep. Her hand rested on my chest. Her body was wrapped in a white sheet, but one leg stretched over it seductively. Seeing such a sight made me feel aroused. It took a lot of effort to calm myself. I couldn't be that selfish. I had to let her rest. Let her sleep. Last night had clearly not been a restful night. Though wildly passionate. I smiled at the thought. A couple of days ago, we didn't even know we existed, and now… I could hardly live a minute without her.

"What are you smiling about?" asked Lacey sleepily.

I looked at her. And even after sleep, she was beautiful.

"I remember… What happened that night…"

"Uh-oh." She buried her head in the pillow. "Now I'm a little embarrassed."

"I didn't feel that way last night." I winked at her.

"You go." She poked me in the shoulder with her elbow. "That's not what I meant. It's just, doesn't it seem too frivolous... Like this, after the first day we met..."

"Hmmm... As it turns out, we've known each other for more than a day."

I turned on my side and propped my head up with my hand.

"You know what?" I asked, watching her brown hair frame her face beautifully.

"What?"

"I envy you..."

"Why?"

"Yesterday you said you saw everything, how we met, how we spent time together... I'm a little sorry I can't see that..."

"You were beautiful even then," she laughed. "You don't have to worry about that."

She, too, rolled over on her side and looked at me.

"Listen! I've been thinking! What if... Well, I'm kind of a trained witch now, right?"

"Yeah..."

"I remembered. I saw these pictures from the past when I was holding your hand... Maybe that's how it works? Maybe we should try it."

Without waiting for my answer, she grabbed my hand.

"Come on! Come on! Do those things with your eyes!"

I just sighed. Okay. After all, nothing bad would happen... I took a deep breath...

"Well? What? Do you see something?"

"No, nothing… I guess…"

I didn't get a chance to finish. A sudden flash cut me off in mid-sentence.

In a second I was in a clearing near a lake. There were two people there. The boy was lying on the girl's lap, looking up at her.

"How do you know?" the girl asked with a smile and ran her hand gently over his cheek.

"I know what I'm saying. We werewolves feel it. You are my true mate. Now we will be together forever. Do you have something against it?"

"No." She continued smiling. "But I was just wondering how you knew that."

"When I look at you, I want to be with you all the time, to hold you, to touch you… When you're away, it's like I'm incomplete… I want to share one breath with you… I am sad when you cry. When you rejoice I smile… But not from what's going on. But from the fact that I like your smile."

"Do you think they'll let us be together?" the girl asked sadly.

She pulled back a little and stood up. The guy did the same. He came very close to her and touched his forehead to hers.

"Listen." He almost whispered it. "Lacey, I don't care who says what. I care about you. Just tell me you're ready to be with me to the end, and I'll move mountains, but we'll be together! So tell me, are you with me?"

"Yes," she replied without thinking, "you just don't leave me alone. I'm not me without you…"

"Lacey, Daniel," came a woman's voice from somewhere, "it's time to say goodbye…"

"Here we go," muttered the boy, "here we go…"

"Come on." She took him by the hand. "Let's not get too hot."

They took a couple of steps.

"I'm sick of this!" he suddenly exclaimed. "Let's tell them right now!"

"You what? Do you have any idea what will happen to them?"

"I don't care about that! What does it matter when they find out about it? The sooner the better. Let them get used to the idea that nothing and no one can keep us apart!"

They ran toward the little brick house. I followed the couple. It was a little uncomfortable to watch all this. I was kind of watching… But who? Myself?

Meanwhile, they were approaching the house. Someone inside was yelling and cursing. A second later, onto the porch flew out… Grandfather. His eyes were filled with rage. I'd never seen him like that before. Well… the part where I hadn't been so ruthlessly wiped out…

After him came running out of the house… Stefania.

"Look, Fred! It's not what you think!"

"I don't want to hear anything!" yelled Grandfather. His eyes missed the crisp blue spark. "Haven't you had enough of what happened then? Enough! I said you'll do what I say, period!"

"What's going on here? Grandpa?"

"Grandma?"

Stefania and Grandpa only threw slanted barbed glances at each other.

"Dan, we're leaving! And you." He turned to Stefania. "Are going to do what we talked about today! Otherwise I'll make the elders reconsider the free existence of witches in Adamantha!"

Grandfather tugged on the boy's arm and led the way.

"Damn you, Fred! You and your whole family! Don't you dare show your face here again! Forget the road to our house."

I opened my eyes. Lacey was still holding my hand.

"Well? Did it work?"

"Yeah." I shook my head, shaking the rest of the vision away from me.

I even wondered for a second if I should have brought it all up. It turns out that Stefania and my grandfather just betrayed us. They were the ones who had contributed to the way things had turned out. What a cruel and incomprehensible world this is!

"Hey." Lacey stroked my hand clenched into a fist. "What are you doing?"

"I understand why they did it, but. Couldn't they have found another way out? Did you have to pay such a price for it?"

"They must have had their reasons... Wait a minute! You said you knew why they did it."

"Yes. It's probably because of the prophecy. It says that if the guardians collide, darkness will fall upon the world. They will be lost in their senses and unable to secure the portals. And then there's only one way to defeat the darkness."

"Which is?"

"If the guardians give their lives at the rock. Then their powers will unite and it will give the triangle unprecedented protection."

"So they wanted to keep us from dying…"

"So they deprived us of a choice! They condemned us to death…"

CHAPTER 21

"Memories."

"Lacey! Lacey! Who am I talking to? Stop looking at your violets! The guests will be here soon!"

The little girl leaned over to one of the violet bushes in the flowerbed, sucked in the smell with her nose, and ran inside the house.

"Who's coming to see us, Mom?" she fidgeted in her chair while her mother braided her long hair into pigtails "And why are they coming? Will they bring presents? Flowers?"

"You're restless." The woman smiled warmly, weaving a ribbon into her braid. "It's an old friend of Grandma's. He's coming with his son and grandson."

"And who are they? Witches? Like us?"

The woman laughed.

"No, baby, they're werewolves."

"Wow… Real ones? They're… they're like wolves?"

"Yeah. Exactly. Wolves. Just Lacey, behave yourself. And keep your violets out of the guests' heads. Not everyone is so obsessed with flowers."

***

The little boy approached the girl, who was fondly digging in the flower bed.

"What are you doing?" he asked.

"I'm trying to replant this," replied the girl without a trace of embarrassment and shook a violet sprout in front of the boy's nose. "They don't feel well there." She nodded towards the big tree. "They need the sun."

"Can I help you?"

"Of course, come here… oh, your eyes… they are just like violets. It's so beautiful."

Since then, their story began. Daniel's family every year came to Swamphorse. They were friends, but… No one could even imagine what it would develop into.

Every year, Daniel and Lacey became closer to each other. At first they played in Lacey's favorite flowerbed, where the violets were in bloom, and then more and more often they began to run away to the lake. And they sat there for a long time, looking at the quiet mirror of the water and at each other.

At first, they did not understand a little what kind of force it was that so invariably pulled them towards each other. But as they got older, they realized. This is love. True mate. A couple where two are destined for each other by fate…

But their sky was not cloudy for long. Their story has been revealed A huge scandal ensued. Families that have been friends with each other for so many years, despite the difference in species, have become bitter enemies. Only their love remained, which they tried to save...

But that too was taken away from them. Everyone understood that the love of Daniel and Lacey could not be destroyed just like that. The idea to resort to magic belonged to Fred – Daniel's grandfather. Stefania did not want to do this until the last moment, hoping that something else could be invented ... But the old werewolf warrior was unyielding. He forced Stefania to cast a spell that took away their memories. One day, after the ritual, Daniel woke up in Blackbrow not knowing who Lacey was. And she... She went with her parents to Quetown, taking with her only a few flower pots... With violets...

CHAPTER 22

"Basilisk."
L.

Daniel and I got carried away looking into the past. Our sad past. In the end, we decided that this can no longer be changed and we need to take everything from the present. Only after we get to Understone and deal with Greif. This may be our last day for us, but we will spend it together...

Before getting into the car, Daniel kissed me. Sweet, strong and passionate. As if goodbye.

We drove in silence the whole way. The sun was shining with might and main on the street, it was a couple of hours drive to Understone. We got a little excited. Perhaps not all is lost...

But we rejoiced early. In the middle of the highway, the day suddenly turned into night. We were attacked by Shadows. We did not have time to do anything, as they threw us along with the car to the side of the road. Daniel came to his senses first. He unbuckled his belt and helped me unbuckle. Then he pulled us out of the car. We sat behind the car, watching the Shadows rampage around.

"Listen to me," he whispered to me, "you sit here as quiet as a mouse and don't stick your head out until I get back, understand?"

I nodded, trembling.

Daniel turned to step out from behind the car.

"Well, well, well... who's hiding here with us?"

The voice of the speaker seemed strangely familiar to me. Daniel and I looked at each other. The stranger walked slowly in our direction, clearly chasing each step.

First I saw black polished shoes. My gaze rose higher and higher. When I saw the face of a stranger, I could hardly keep myself from screaming.

Leaning right over us... Peter.

"Holy shit," cursed Daniel.

"I'm glad to see you too, friend." Peter winked at us.

"And why are you sitting here? Do you not want to join our fun?" He waved his hand in the direction of the highway.

"God, Pete, who are you?" I exclaimed. I was terribly scared from the realization of the one who all this time was an indispensable assistant in my club...

"Oh... I love this reaction to myself." Peter grinned.

"How?" croaked Daniel. "How did you manage to hide it for so many years?"

"Daniel," drawled Peter, "you're as naive as a child. I didn't hide anything from anyone. Peter Swan is truly your best friend and indispensable companion to Lacey... why he didn't inherit his werewolf father's genes is really a mystery… Just to me a body was needed… a body that did not arouse suspicion.

"What?" I screamed "Who are you? What did you do to Pete?"

I rushed to this monster, but Daniel stopped me.

"Lacey, Peter's not there any more… It's Greif."

"Bravo, Mr. Byne, your insight is on top."

"Listen, there are special forces everywhere. Go back to your gorge and I promise I'll tell the guys not to do anything to you."

"How nice… Daniel Byne himself is doing me a favor." Greif laughed wickedly.

"Or maybe…" Greif came very close to us and said almost in a whisper, "we won't wait for anyone? Let's solve this issue here and now?"

He straightened up, his eyes began to redden, and his face contorted into an ugly grimace. The clothes began to split at the seams. What was Peter's body transformed in the blink of an eye into a creepy thing with a snake's body and a rooster's head.

Wings sprouted from his back. Greif soared above us and flashed his red eyes.

"Gosh, who is this?" I whispered.

"Basilisk. Greif is also a shifter. But he doesn't turn into a wolf."

"Basilisk? But…"

"Harry Potter was very different, right?" Daniel chuckled. "I already told you. You think too stereotypically… Basilisk – this is it, its true face."

Ordering me to be quiet, Daniel also took off his mask. Now in front of Greif stood a formidable black wolf. A fight began not for life, but for death, they mercilessly struck each other, but I prayed for only one thing, that Daniel would survive and this crazy man would not hurt him badly.

I did not notice how the Shadow flew up to me. She instantly enveloped me and began to choke me. I only had time to let out a short squeak. But this turned out to be a fatal mistake. Hearing me, Daniel turned around and twitched in my direction. This moment was enough for Greif to contrive and slash Daniel's stomach with his sharp tail. Emitting the heartbreaking howl of a wounded beast, Daniel fell to the ground. It seems to me that then I screamed with my eyes, because the Shadow squeezed my throat.

"Ah, love… I always said it doesn't do any good." Greif transformed again and loomed over me as Peter.

"Well, Lacey, come with me." He grinned nastily again and walked forward. The Shadow dragged me after him.

"And take this dog away. We'll still need it."

CHAPTER 23

"I Don't Need the Whole World."
L.

I opened my eyes and saw the sky above me. Dark sky with black storm clouds. I was lying somewhere in the meadow. I tried to get up. After several attempts, I succeeded, despite the fact that my hands were tied. I looked ahead. My gaze caught on a huge stone that stood in the middle of the clearing. But that wasn't what scared me the most. Beneath the stone, crouched in an unnatural position, lay Daniel. His eyes were closed. I couldn't tell if he was breathing or not. I screamed.

"What did you do to him?"

"Lace, leave it. Daniel is resting." Grinning nastily, Peter walked up to Daniel and patted his cheek.

"If you remember, we had a little fight... I didn't think it would be so serious."

With a quick movement, Peter lifted Daniel's T-shirt. His tattoo was crossed in a large bloody trail.

"Dany must have told you that werewolves heal quickly. There's just one caveat. If his tattoo is torn off...

Then… Healing can be very very, very slow… Or not at all."

"What do you want? What do you need? Leave him, let him heal! You need me! Look, I'm not even resisting!"

I jerked forward, trying to get up.

"What nobility. Do you think he deserves such a sacrifice? Don't answer though. You and your true mate are doomed. I just want to have some fun… Hey, Dany…"

Greif walked up to Daniel and kicked him hard in the stomach. Daniel writhed in pain. For a second, his eyes opened. I saw that long-awaited violet color again. He was alive. God bless. But what Greif did made me angry. I don't know where I got so much strength from. Screaming, I tensed my arms. In a second, I managed to break the ropes that tied my hands.

It was as if the wind had taken over me.

"Get away from him!" I threw my hand forward.

I could see how a powerful air wave swept from me to Greif. It only shook him a little. But Greif just laughed.

"You are still so stupid, Lacey. All of you are fools who are guided by emotions. You have driven yourself into a trap. Now you are at your best. And that means it's time to start the final act of our play."

With those words, Greif began to transform into an ugly basilisk. Making a piercing sound, more like a grinding of metal, he flew up to the stone and raised his muzzle to the sky. His eyes turned into bright beams that attracted lightning. All this was accompanied by wind and wild sound.

Fighting the wind, I crawled over to Daniel and cupped his face in my hands.

"Dan, Dan, wake up... Dan, please! You promised you wouldn't leave me alone! Please! Dan."

I patted his face. A cough escaped his throat. He finally opened his eyes. His bleary gaze barely focused on me. He curved his lips into what looked like a smile.

"Maybe we really were doomed," he croaked, "but I'm glad that I will leave this life, having seen the most beautiful in the end."

"No, no, no... you're not leaving... No, do you hear me? There must be a way out... Stefania said something about blood on the stone... How is it? You are one... Blood on the stone shed light.. You are one... You are... Yes! Dan! Dan! I know how to save us! Dan, can you hear me?"

He slowly turned his head towards me.

I sincerely hope that I was not mistaken and this will help. I rummaged through the grass with my hand and found a small stone with a pointed end. I brought it to my hand and pressed hard.

"What are you doing, Lace?"

It hurt like hell, but I got my way. A crimson trickle of blood appeared on the palm of his hand.

"Trust me. Stefania believed in us. She gave us a clue."

I brought my hand up to Daniel's. He still had blood from Greif's wound. I connected our hands and brought them to the stone. Our hands were imprinted on the surface in a bloody trail, but nothing else happened …

What? No… Am I wrong? No, it can't end like this… We don't…

Suddenly, the ground shook beneath us. Holes began to appear on the huge stone, through which huge beams of light made their way. There were more and more rays. They turned into one continuous bright canvas of light. This light engulfed Greif at the top of the stone. Letting out a terrifying screech, Greif completely disappeared into the light. And then followed by an explosion of crushing force. And silence. I leaned over Daniel and closed my eyes. I was afraid to open them because I didn't know what I could see. But suddenly Daniel was moving nearby. I made up my mind anyway. We were still at the rock, but… The sky was crystal blue, without a single charge. The grass in the clearing shone with dew like emeralds… And yet… There were violets everywhere… many violets…

"Dan? Are you with me? Dan?"

Daniel slowly opened his eyes.

"I'm here."

I hugged him tightly, feeling tears roll down my face.

"God, I was so scared! I thought I lost you! How are you? Does it hurt somewhere?"

I yanked down his shirt. There was no trace of Greif's wound. Daniel's tattoo has almost healed.

"Dan! We won, you hear? We won! We saved the world."

He pulled me towards him.

"I don't know about the world, but I definitely hit the jackpot."

He flashed his violet eyes at me and kissed me...

THE END

FROM THE AUTHOR

This book was written in the spring of 2022, against the backdrop of the events that took place in my country, Ukraine, at that time. It is about Russia's brutal, bloody, and insidious attack on Ukraine.

The story is not based on real events, this work highlights some particularly vivid moments of the Russian-Ukrainian war and is adapted to the fantasy genre.

The plot is built on a play on words, translation and prototypes.

For example, Adamantha is a country of the unconquered, which is actually a model of Ukraine. Blackbrow is one of the cities of Adamantha, like the famous Ukrainian Chornobaivka (a small town in the Kherson region where the occupiers repeatedly attacked but were kicked in the teeth by the Ukrainian soldiers, who even kept track of how many times they were defeated). Daniel Byne is a resident of Blackbrow, a soldier of the Special Operations Forces, and a werewolf. His image was created on the basis of legends about an ancient family of Cossack characters who were very strong and turned into wolves. It is in Chornobaivka that their story begins.

Swamphorse is the second city featured in the novel. Its prototype is the Ukrainian town of Konotop. Konotop is located in the Sumy region, on the border with Russia. Since ancient times, Konotop has had a mystical reputation. Namely, it was associated with witches. There was a large concentration of them in Konotop. There is even a stable expression 'Konotop witch'. It was she who became one of the characters in the novel.

Understone, the prototype of the town of Pidkamin in the Lviv region. There is a huge stone here. According to the legend, the devil was angry with the monks and decided to turn the mountain into a city. But he only had enough strength for a rock. Actually, the stone has this name: 'Devil's Roc'.

And Quetown is Kyiv, the capital of Ukraine. A big, bustling metropolis, the heart of a strong and unbreakable state.

And it will not be difficult for the reader to draw parallels between the Dark Forces and the main villain, the king of the Dark Kingdom, Greif Volturis...

I hope that this work will find its reader, and this peculiar presentation of the difficult period of my country will be my personal contribution to the victory not only of Ukraine, but of the world as a whole, in the fight against the terrorist country...